Second Look by

Kathi Daley

This book is a work of fiction. Names, characters, places, and incidents either are products of the author's imagination or are used fictitiously. Any resemblance to actual events or locales or persons, living or dead, is entirely coincidental.

Version 1.0

I want to thank the very talented Jessica Fischer for the cover art.

I so appreciate Bruce Curran, who is always ready and willing to answer my cyber questions, and Peggy Hyndman for helping sleuth out those pesky typos.

And, of course, thanks to the readers and bloggers in my life, who make doing what I do possible.

Thank you to Randy Ladenheim-Gil for the editing.

And finally I want to thank my sister Christy for always lending an ear and my husband Ken for allowing me time to write by taking care of everything else.

Books by Kathi Daley

Come for the murder, stay for the romance.

Zoe Donovan Cozy Mystery:

Halloween Hijinks
The Trouble With Turkeys
Christmas Crazy
Cupid's Curse
Big Bunny Bump-off
Beach Blanket Barbie
Maui Madness
Derby Divas
Haunted Hamlet
Turkeys, Tuxes, and Tabbies
Christmas Cozy
Alaskan Alliance
Matrimony Meltdown
Soul Surrender
Heavenly Honeymoon
Hopscotch Homicide
Ghostly Graveyard
Santa Sleuth
Shamrock Shenanigans
Kitten Kaboodle
Costume Catastrophe
Candy Cane Caper
Holiday Hangover
Easter Escapade
Camp Carter
Trick or Treason – *September 2017*
Reindeer Roundup – *December 2017*

Zimmerman Academy The New Normal
Ashton Falls Cozy Cookbook

Tj Jensen Paradise Lake Mysteries by Henery Press

Pumpkins in Paradise
Snowmen in Paradise
Bikinis in Paradise
Christmas in Paradise
Puppies in Paradise
Halloween in Paradise
Treasure in Paradise
Fireworks in Paradise – *October 2017*

Whales and Tails Cozy Mystery:

Romeow and Juliet
The Mad Catter
Grimm's Furry Tail
Much Ado About Felines
Legend of Tabby Hollow
Cat of Christmas Past
A Tale of Two Tabbies
The Great Catsby
Count Catula
The Cat of Christmas Present
A Winter's Tail
The Taming of the Tabby
Frankencat – *August 2017*
The Cat of Christmas Future – *November 2017*

Seacliff High Mystery:

The Secret
The Curse
The Relic
The Conspiracy
The Grudge
The Shadow
The Haunting – *September 2017*

Sand and Sea Hawaiian Mystery:

Murder at Dolphin Bay
Murder at Sunrise Beach
Murder at the Witching Hour
Murder at Christmas
Murder at Turtle Cove
Murder at Water's Edge
Murder at Midnight – *October 2017*

Writers' Retreat Southern Seashore Mystery:

First Case
Second Look
Third Strike
Fourth Victim – *October 2017*

Rescue Alaska Paranormal Mystery

Finding Justice – *November 2017*

Road to Christmas Romance:

Road to Christmas Past

The Writers:

Jillian (Jill) Hanford

Jillian is a dark-haired, dark-eyed, never-married thirty-eight-year-old newspaper reporter who moved to Gull Island after her much-older brother, Garrett Hanford, had a stroke and was no longer able to run the resort he'd inherited. Jillian had suffered a personal setback and needed a change in lifestyle, so she decided to run the resort as a writers' retreat while she waited for an opportunity to work her way back into her old life. To help make ends meet, she takes on freelance work that allows her to maintain her ties to the newspaper industry. Jillian shares her life with her partner in mystery solving, an ornery parrot with an uncanny ability to communicate named Blackbeard.

Jackson (Jack) Jones

Jack is a dark-haired, blue-eyed, never-married forty-two-year-old nationally acclaimed author of hard-core mysteries and thrillers, who is as famous for his good looks and boyish charm as he is for the stories he pens. Despite his success as a novelist, he'd always dreamed of writing for a newspaper, so he gave up his penthouse apartment and bought the failing *Gull Island News*. He lives in an oceanfront mansion he pays for with income from the novels he continues to write.

George Baxter

George is a sixty-eight-year-old writer of traditional whodunit mysteries. He'd been a friend of Garrett Hanford's since they were boys and spent many winters at the resort penning his novels. When he heard that the oceanfront resort was going to be used as a writers' retreat, he was one of the first to get on board. George is a distinguished-looking man with gray hair, dark green eyes, and a certain sense of old-fashioned style that many admire.

Clara Kline

Clara is a sixty-two-year-old, self-proclaimed psychic who writes fantasy and paranormal mysteries. She wears her long gray hair in a practical braid and favors long, peasant-type skirts and blouses. Clara decided to move to the retreat after she had a vision that she would find her soul mate living within its walls. So far, the only soul mate she has stumbled on to is a cat named Agatha, but it does seem that romance is in the air, so she may yet find the man she has envisioned.

Alex Cole

Alex is a twenty-eight-year-old, fun and flirty millennial who made his first million writing science fiction when he was just twenty-two. He's the lighthearted jokester of the group who uses his blond-haired, blue-eyed good looks to participate in serial dating. He has the means to live anywhere, but the thought of a writers' retreat seemed quaint and retro, so he decided to expand his base of experience and moved in.

Brit Baxter

Brit is George Baxter's twenty-six-year-old niece. A petite blond pixie, she decided to make the trip east with her uncle after quitting her job to pursue her dream of writing. She's an MIT graduate who decided her real love was writing.

Victoria Vance

Victoria is a thirty-seven-year-old romance author who lives the life she writes about in her steamy novels. She travels the world and does what she wants to who she wants without ever making an emotional connection. Her raven-black hair accentuates her pale skin and bright green eyes. She's the woman every man fantasizes about but none can ever conquer. When she isn't traveling the world, she's Jillian's best friend, which is why when Jillian needed her, she gave up her penthouse apartment overlooking Central Park to move into the dilapidated island retreat.

Townsfolk:

Deputy Rick Savage

Rick is not only the island's main source of law enforcement, he's a volunteer force unto himself. He cares about the island and its inhabitants and is willing to do what needs to be done to protect that which he loves. He's a single man in his thirties who seldom has time to date despite his devilish good looks, which most believe could land him any woman he wants.

Mayor Betty Sue Bell

Betty Sue is a homegrown Southern lady who owns a beauty parlor called Betty Boop's Beauty Salon. She can be flirty and sassy, but when her town or its citizens are in trouble, she turns into a barracuda. She has a southern flare that will leave you laughing, but when there's a battle to fight she's the one you most want in your corner.

Gertie Newsome

Gertie Newsome is the owner of Gertie's on the Wharf. Southern born and bred, she believes in the magic of the South and the passion of its people. She shares her home with a ghost named Mortie who has been a regular part of her life for over thirty years. She's friendly, gregarious, and outspoken, unafraid to take on anyone or anything she needs to protect those she loves.

Meg Collins

Meg is a sixty-six-year-old volunteer at the island museum and the organizer of the turtle rescue squad. Some feel the island and its wildlife are her life, but Meg has a soft spot for island residents like Jill and the writers who live with her.

Barbara Jean Freeman

Barbara is an outspoken woman with a tendency toward big hair and loud colors. She's a friendly sort with a propensity toward gossip who owns a bike shop in town.

Sully

Sully is a popular islander who owns the local bar.

The Victims and Suspects

Georgia Darcy – Hillary Crawford's younger sister and the victim
Dru Breland – Georgia's date and the assumed killer
Rhett Crawford – The host – A famous movie star who owned a beach house on the island
Hillary Crawford – The hostess and Rhett's wife
Jedd Boswell – Rhett's best friend who lived in Hollywood and was also an actor
Honey Golden – Jedd's date, who lived in Los Angeles and worked as a model
Tiffany Pritchett – A friend of Hillary's who lives on the island
Reggie Southern – Tiffany's date, who also lived on the island
Claudia Norris – The next-door neighbor to the beach house
Trent Truitt – Also a resident of Gull Island and Claudia's date
Olivia Cotton – The cook hired to help for the long weekend
Wiley Slater – The groundskeeper who lived on the estate

Chapter 1

Monday, October 23

Five years ago, award-winning actor Rhett Crawford threw a party for a group of family members and friends. The event was held at his beachfront estate on Gull Island. At around eleven-thirty on the night of the party, the groundskeeper, Wylie Slater, found the body of one of the guests, Georgia Darcy, bludgeoned to death and left in the toolshed at the edge of the property, beyond the garden. The authorities were notified and interviews of all individuals on the property were conducted. It was eventually determined that the victim's date, a man named Dru Breland, had most likely killed the woman before fleeing the scene of the crime.

After Georgia's remains were found, the authorities conducted an exhaustive search but were unable to locate Mr. Breland. As far as anyone associated with the investigation could find out, he was never seen again by friends, family, or business associates. It was assumed by most that he had fled the country and started a new life under an assumed name.

Then, five days ago, the oceanfront estate once owned by Rhett Crawford but now owned by an out-of-state developer, was scheduled for demolition. During the destruction of the house, a human skeleton was found in a hidden room off the wine cellar. After a thorough investigation by the medical examiner and his team, it was determined that the body was the decomposed remains of murder suspect Dru Breland.

My friend Jackson Jones, owner of the fledging *Gull Island News*, had latched onto the story and seemed determined to find out not only how Dru Breland ended up in the secret room but who had killed Georgia Darcy, if, in fact, Dru Breland wasn't the killer, as everyone had believed. Jack knew the five-year-old mystery would be a complicated one to unravel, so he asked me, Jillian Hanford, if I'd be willing to present it to the writers' group I lived and sleuthed with. I agreed, which brings us to the regular Monday night meeting of the eclectic group of writers I call friends but consider family.

"Okay, so what do we know about the other guests at the party?" asked George Baxter, a sixty-eight-year-old writer of traditional whodunits who was currently living in one of the cabins on the property I was running as a writers' retreat.

"There were twelve people in all on the property during the party," Jack answered. "As I mentioned before, the estate was owned by actor Rhett Crawford. He, along with his wife at the time, Hillary Crawford, invited eight guests, including four visitors from off the island: the victim, Georgia Darcy, who was Hillary Crawford's younger sister; Georgia's date, Dru Breland, who was living in Los Angeles at that time; Jedd Boswell, also an actor and Rhett's best friend; and Honey Golden, a model living in Orange County and Jedd's date."

Jack paused while I wrote the names of the out-of-town guests on the whiteboard we always used when attempting to unravel mysteries. We'd found visuals to be invaluable as relationships, motives, and secrets long kept began to reveal themselves.

"Also at the party were six Gull Island residents," Jack continued. "Tiffany Pritchett, a friend of Hillary's; Reggie Southern, Tiffany's date; Claudia Norris, the woman who owned the adjoining estate and had become friendly with the Crawfords, and her date, Trent Truitt; and two employees, Olivia Cotton, who was hired to handle the cooking, and Wylie Slater, who lived on the property and worked as the groundskeeper."

Once all the players had been identified, Jack paused to ask if there were any questions. I glanced around the room, which was lit by a crackling fire and warm candlelight. On this particular occasion, the electricity was up and running, but after a previous meeting held during a blackout caused by a storm, we'd decided the subdued lighting somehow heightened the senses. The only electric light in the room was a small overhead one we'd positioned over the whiteboard so everyone could see the details I was recording.

"I'm not really one to keep up on all the Hollywood news," Clara Kline, a sixty-two-year-old, self-proclaimed psychic who wrote fantasy and paranormal mysteries, admitted. "You said Hillary

Crawford was married to Rhett Crawford at the time of the murder. Have they since dissolved their relationship?"

"Yes," Jack answered. "They were divorced shortly after the murder of Hillary's sister, Georgia. The specifics of their divorce aren't public record, but the press at the time reported that Hillary in some way blamed Rhett for what happened to Georgia."

"Did they have children?"

Jack shook his head. "The couple seemed to be focused on their careers above all else. Not only was Rhett a major star at the time of the party but Hillary was a pretty big name as well. Based on what I've heard, it seems the couple's relationship took a backseat to the fame they seemed to crave."

Clara rocked back and forth in the antique rocker she favored, stroking her cat, Agatha, but not commenting further. Clara was an intuitive of sorts who had, in the past, helped provide key pieces of information necessary to solve the mysteries we were working on. The problem was, she was an emotionally intense individual who had a tendency to be flighty and distracted. When her emotions became too entangled with the specifics of the case, they seemed to block the psychic ability she claimed to possess. I just hoped she'd be able to maintain an emotional distance and help us out this time.

"Do we know if any of the guests who attended the party still live on Gull Island?" asked Brit Baxter, George's twenty-six-year-old niece and the newest resident at my writers' retreat. Brit had been a business major who'd decided her true calling was to be a writer. She'd yet to have anything published, but she'd already established herself as a valuable member of our little family. She had an intense look of concentration on her face as she sat on a barstool next to where the resident mascot, a parrot named Blackbeard, watched from his perch.

"Tiffany, Claudia, Olivia, and Wylie still live on the island," Jack answered. "Tiffany Pritchett, who, as you'll remember, was Hillary's friend, is married to a contractor, Vince Flannigan. The couple have two children and seem to be contributing members of the Gulf Island community. Olivia Cotton, the woman hired to cook for the party, now owns her own bakery in town, and Wylie Slater, the Crawfords' groundskeeper, now owns a fishing boat docked in the marina. And finally, Claudia Norris, who lived next door to the Crawfords' beach house, still lives on the same property. She's single and is no longer dating Trent Truitt."

"And Truitt?" Brit asked.

"Now lives on Folly Island." Jack named a nearby island.

"So it seems Tiffany, Claudia, Olivia, Wylie, and Trent should be available to interview," stated Alex Cole, a twenty-eight-year-old, fun and flirty millennial who'd made his first million writing science fiction when he was just twenty-two.

"In terms of proximity, it seems very likely these individuals will be available for interviews," Jack agreed. "I haven't, however, had the opportunity to contact any of them, so it remains to be seen whether they'll be willing to share their memories of what occurred."

"I don't see why they wouldn't speak to us if they're innocent," Alex added. "If they're guilty of killing two people, however…"

Alex made a good point. If Dru hadn't killed Georgia, one of the people we sought to interview most likely had.

"So where do we start?" Brit asked.

"Is everyone in to help?" Jack queried.

"As interesting as this sounds, I'm heading to New York tomorrow morning," Alex informed us. "I have meetings with my agent, publicist, and publisher, so I'll be gone for four or five days. If you haven't solved this by the time I return, I'd be happy to help then."

"Actually," Jack smiled, "the fact that you're heading to New York works out really well. I did some research before this meeting, and it seems Hillary Crawford moved to Manhattan after she divorced Rhett. I have her current address and phone number. Maybe you can find the time to interview her while you're there."

"I'd be happy to." Alex reached out for the paper on which Jack had recorded Hillary's contact information. "I'll call you to let you know what I find out."

"What about the others who aren't on the island?" I asked. "Do you know where they are now?"

"Rhett and Jedd still live in Los Angeles. They both continue to be active in the entertainment industry. Reggie Southern, Tiffany's date to the party, has moved to Charleston."

"And Honey Golden?" I asked.

"Her present whereabouts are unknown."

"I'll do some research to see if I can track her down," Brit volunteered. "Almost everyone has social media accounts these days. I'm sure I can find her, and maybe Victoria can have a chat with Rhett and Jedd."

"I'll call to ask her," I said.

Victoria Vance was the final member of our writers' group, a thirty-seven-year-old romance writer who lives the life she writes about in her steamy novels. She was currently in Los Angeles, meeting with the production studio that was thinking of making some of her novels into movies. She'd be the perfect person to interview Rhett and Jedd. For one thing, she possessed certain assets that tended to make men do whatever she asked of them. For another, Victoria is a strong-willed woman who rarely takes no for an answer.

"Jill and I will get started on the interviews for the guests living in the area," Jack added. "I have contact information for most of them and should be able to dig up phone numbers for the rest."

I glanced at Clara, who seemed to be deep in thought. "Are you picking up anything?" I asked.

She frowned. "Maybe, but I'm not ready to say anything just yet. When we're done here, I'll consult my cards to see if I can confirm my suspicions."

I was happy to see Clara was on board and hoped she'd be able to make a connection.

"And I'll look in to the history of the estate," George offered. "The idea of a secret room intrigues me. I wonder if its existence was widely known."

"If not, that could narrow down our suspect list," Jack said.

"It would be interesting to find out if the room was built into the original structure of the house or if Rhett added it." George looked at Jack. "Do you happen to know if there was anything in the room other than the body of Dru Breland?"

"I'm not sure. I'll see if I can find out."

"How long ago was the property sold to the developer?" George added.

"I think about a year ago," Jack answered. "I'll find out the exact date."

"On the surface, it seems Rhett is a likely suspect because he would know about the room, but if he's the one who put the body in it, I would think he'd have moved it before he sold the property. He was selling to a developer, so he must have figured the house would be torn down at some point."

George might be right. In all likelihood, Rhett wasn't the killer.

The room fell into silence. I glanced at Blackbeard, who seemed to be taking in everything that was happening and was watching, not speaking. I know looking to a bird for insight might seem odd, but I've discovered since living on the island that Blackbeard had a way of knowing exactly what was going on even when no one else had a clue.

"Does Deputy Savage know you're taking a second look at the case?" George asked Jack.

I glanced at Jack. I'd wondered that myself but hadn't gotten around to asking. Deputy Savage was a good guy who honestly seemed to care about the people he had sworn to serve, but he hadn't been much of a fan of civilians getting involved in ongoing cases. While the case had been closed when it had been decided that Dru Breland must have murdered Georgia Darcy, there hadn't been an ongoing investigation. I was certain it would be reopened now that Breland's body had been found.

"I haven't spoken to Deputy Savage, so I don't know what he thinks about the new developments in the case," Jack admitted. "Having said that, I'm a newspaperman now and it's my duty to my readers to find and report the facts as I see them. I believe we all have our assignments. When should we meet again?"

"I can meet whenever," Brit answered. "When's Victoria due back?"

"I don't think until the weekend at least," I told her. "But she can pass along anything she finds out to me and I'll bring it to the meeting."

"I won't be back for several days, but I'm fine with calling Jack or Jill with any information I uncover as well," Alex added.

I glanced at George, who asked for a day or so to do his research but was pretty open, and Clara indicated her schedule was flexible as well. Those of us who would be on the island tentatively arranged to meet again on Thursday. George, Brit, and Alex headed out to the cabins they were living in and Clara and Agatha went upstairs to her suite.

I began picking up coffee mugs and dessert plates once they'd gone and it was just Jack and me. "So what do you think?" I asked.

"I think we have a good plan that hopefully will yield the results we need. We won't begin to get a good picture of what might have occurred five years ago until we begin to speak to people. I can make some calls in the morning and set up appointments if you want to get started right away."

"Yeah. We may as well plunge right in." I glanced at Blackbeard. "Any thoughts?"

"Secret kisses, secret kisses."

“That, big guy, turns out to be the motive behind more murders than you might think,” Jack replied.

I opened Blackbeard’s cage. “How about we get you settled in for the night?” I turned and glanced at Jack. “I have wine in the kitchen if you want to stay.”

“I have an article to write, but we’ll catch up tomorrow. Call me and we’ll set up a time to get started on the interviews.”

After Jack left, I got Blackbeard settled and then poured myself a glass of wine. It was a lovely autumn evening and a stroll along the beach seemed just the thing to sooth my jangled nerves. The last time the group had taken on a case it had been at my request, and the time before that it had been George we’d helped. When I’d decided to move to Gull Island temporarily to help the half brother I hadn’t known I had, I’d never imagined the family I’d find; not just Garrett, but the writers I shared my life with as well.

The idea for the writers’ retreat had been something of a whim. Garrett had run the place as a family resort before he’d had his stroke. When he realized he would most likely never be able to live on his own again, he’d thought he had no choice but to sell the property that had been in his family for generations. The resort had fallen into disrepair over the past decade, and Garrett realized that to make any money selling the resort he’d have to fix it up first. Initially, he’d asked an old friend of the family to oversee the renovations, but when a chance occurrence revealed my existence to him, he’d gotten in touch and asked me if I’d be willing to run the property in his absence. Normally, island living wouldn’t be my thing, but my own life was a total mess at that time, and I'd jumped at the chance to escape and try something new.

I walked along the well-worn path to the beach. The Turtle Cove Resort was a magical place, situated on the tip of a narrow peninsula that jetted off the southern end of Gull Island. Due to its unique location, the property was bordered by oceanfront on the east and marsh on the west. The sheer amount of wildlife that inhabited this part of the island, including the endangered sea turtles, created an enchanting setting to work and live.

Initially, I'd planned to oversee the renovations and then move on. I could see Garrett wanted me to stay, but I couldn't see myself running a family resort. Then his good friend, George Baxter, had come for a visit, and a conversation about the old days, when he'd come here to write, gave me the idea of reopening the resort as a writers' retreat rather than a family vacation spot. I'd approached Garrett with the idea and he'd assured me that he was fine with my running the property whatever way I saw fit. At that time only the main house was habitable, but it had ten bedrooms, so George had moved in. Shortly after that, Clara found her way to my doorstep, followed by my best friend Victoria, Alex, and, eventually, Brit.

The remodel of three of the cabins was now completed, so George, Alex, and Brit all had their own space. Clara seemed content to remain in the main house, and while Victoria wanted her own cabin eventually, she wasn't around much and so had been content to wait. I'd remodeled the attic to create my own private retreat within the communal structure; so far, my plans were working out perfectly, and I had additional writers who'd signed on to come aboard as soon as the first of the year.

I paused and took a sip of wine as the waves rolled gently onto the shore. It was a cool evening, although the day had been hot, so I took a moment to enjoy the perfection of the moment. It seemed I'd been running full throttle ever since making the decision to move to the island. Not only had I had the renovation to deal with but our little mystery solvers group had been kept quite busy as well.

Jack was the only member of the group who didn't live at the resort, but as a writer, he was qualified for membership. Not only did he own the local newspaper, but he was a novelist, probably more successful than all the rest of us combined.

Jack had written his first best seller and made his first million when he was just nineteen. Since then, he'd had several other best sellers and was considered one of the major names in the industry. He lived in an oceanfront mansion, but most weekday evenings you could find him here at the resort, hanging out with the rest of us lowly writers.

I took a deep breath and turned back to the house. Despite the peaceful evening, I had a bad feeling in the pit of my stomach. I couldn't imagine how investigating a five-year-old murder could put anyone in danger, but my instinct told me it would be found before the answers we sought were revealed.

Chapter 2

Tuesday, October 24

I woke before the sun was in the sky the next morning. It was cool and crisp, which I greatly appreciated after the long, hot summer. I pulled on jeans and a sweatshirt and headed out for a walk on the beach. I was just about to close the back door behind me when Agatha scooted out between my legs and scampered to a location several steps ahead of me.

"Does Clara know you plan to come with me?"

"Meow."

Given the fact that Clara was a self-proclaimed psychic, I supposed I should assume she knew her cat had chosen to join me on my walk, but I didn't want her to wake up and worry, so I headed back inside, jotted down a quick note, and attached it to the coffeemaker. Then I headed back outdoors, where Agatha was waiting for me.

"The sun should be up in a few minutes," I said aloud as I headed toward the beach on the east side of the peninsula, where the resort was located.

I'd very much enjoyed watching the sun rise as well as set since I'd been living on the island. When I lived in New York, I spent most of my time indoors, and the passage of time seemed to blur from one day into the next. Since I'd moved to Gull Island, I tried to take in as many beginnings and endings of the day as I could manage.

Once Agatha and I reached the sand we walked to the south. The turtles who came to the island to lay their eggs every year had gone and the eggs that had survived had hatched. I found I missed the turtles and was looking forward to their return in the spring. Every aspect of my life seemed to have changed since I'd moved to the island. I still missed the hustle and bustle of my old life at times, but I found that my desire to return to what had been seemed to slip away just a bit more with each passing day.

I paused to enjoy the foliage, which was beginning to turn. The oranges, reds, and yellows displayed by the deciduous trees were breathtaking. I'd always enjoyed the fall colors but had never taken a lot of time to seek it out. There was something about the majesty of a South Carolina fall, however, that had me thinking of decorating my little resort with pumpkins, scarecrows, and everything autumn.

"Perhaps we should have a Halloween party this year," I said to Agatha. "Nothing too elaborate, just some food, drink, and good friends. We can invite Jack and the rest of the gang and maybe a few people from town."

"Meow."

"Yes, I did remember the harvest festival is this weekend. Maybe a small dinner party on the thirty-first."

When I'd lived in New York I had a tiny apartment, so I never entertained much and never bothered to decorate for the various seasons and holidays. Now that I had a real home, with plenty of room, the idea of hosting a holiday party grew on me more and more the longer I thought about it. I stopped walking as the first rays of the morning sun peeked over the horizon. As many times as I watched the sun rise over the ocean, it was an experience I'd never tire of. There was something about the birth of a new day that sent chills through my body. I sat down on the sand and cuddled Agatha to my chest as the sun continued its ascent.

I tried to relax and enjoy the beauty of the morning, but I found I was anxious about the day ahead. I loved a juicy mystery, and the one Jack had presented seemed to be of the very juiciest variety, but I felt a bit of trepidation as well. I couldn't quite put my finger on what was bothering me, but I found a heaviness had descended on my shoulders. It could be that life in general had been busy as of late, but somehow, I didn't think that was quite it. I took a breath and closed my eyes as I tried to focus my thoughts. I couldn't decide what it was that was causing my anxiety, which probably meant that any angst I was feeling was simply a product of my mind.

I opened my eyes and looked once again at the rising sun. I had so much to be happy about. So many blessings in my life. I hugged Agatha just a bit tighter and smiled at the birth of the new day. Once the sun was fully exposed, I set the cat on the sand, stood up, and started back toward the house to get ready for the day ahead.

******

I made breakfast for Clara, George, and myself, then took a shower, dressed in clean jeans and a warm burnt-orange-colored sweater, and headed into town. I'd arranged to meet Jack in less than an hour, but I wanted to stop by the general store first to pick up some pumpkins and fall accents for the front porch.

"Morning, Cliff," I greeted the tall, thin man with light-colored hair that was beginning to bald.

"Mornin', Jill. Batteries are on sale today and I have a new shipment of winter blankets in stock."

"I'm good on blankets and batteries, but I've decided to decorate, so I've come in search of pumpkins and any other fall accents you have in stock."

"Pumpkins are out back in the nursery. Small ones are three dollars and big ones are five. We also have candles, garlands, and other fall and Halloween decorations in aisle twelve. The ceramic pumpkins have been real popular, as have the silk flower arrangements."

"Thanks. I'll take a look to see what catches my eye." I grabbed a basket and headed to aisle twelve. I figured I'd get whatever I needed from inside the store and then go out for the pumpkins.

The holiday decorations were creating a warm, fuzzy feeling I hadn't had for quite some time. To be honest, in the past I'd never really paid much attention to the holidays. My mom was never around and I didn't have any other family with whom to celebrate. Of course, I had a few friends, and they all had family events to which I'd been invited, though I'd never attended. I couldn't remember the last time I'd been as excited as I was this year for any holiday to arrive.

I'd almost filled my basket completely before I made my way to the end of aisle twelve. I'd decided to leave the full cart in the front of the store and get a new one for the pumpkins. I'd just parked the first basket when I bumped into Gertie Newsome, the owner of one of my favorite restaurants, Gertie's on the Wharf.

"Looks like someone's been bitten by the Halloween bug." Gertie chuckled, taking in my overflowing basket.

I grinned in return. "Yes, I guess I have. It's been a long time since I've celebrated any holiday, but I find I'm very much looking forward to my first one in my new home."

"We do holidays big here on Gull Island," Gertie informed me. "You plannin' to come to the harvest festival this weekend?"

"I wouldn't miss it. I've even volunteered to work in the snack shack for a few hours on Sunday. By the way, I was thinking of having a small dinner party on Halloween night. Nothing fancy. Maybe fondue. I'd love for you to come if you aren't busy."

Gertie laughed. "Well, I was planning to stay home and share ghost stories with Mortie, but dinner with you all sounds a lot livelier."

I had to roll my eyes at Gertie's play on words. Mortie was the ghost who had lived in her house for the past thirty years. Or at least that was what Gertie told everyone. I was withholding judgment at the moment, though Mortie had come up with some key insights when I was investigating our last mystery.

"Great. I need to check with the others, but why don't you plan to come by at around six?"

"Will do, suga. Oh, and as long as I ran into you, I have a message from Mortie."

"What sort of message?"

"He said to tell you the man in the room hasn't been there since the night that young woman was killed."

"He hasn't? Did Mortie say how long he *had* been there?"

Gertie shook her head. "He wasn't specific with his dates; he just indicated that the two murders didn't occur on the same night, as most assume."

If Mortie was real *and* could communicate with Gertie *and* his intel was correct, the fact that Dru was murdered at some point after Georgia's death could be a vital clue to what had occurred. When Jack had told us that Dru's body had been found hidden in a secret room on the same estate where Georgia's body had been found, I'd just assumed that meant he hadn't killed Georgia but had been killed by the same person who'd ended her life.

"Did Mortie happen to mention who might have killed either Dru or Georgia?"

"He didn't say. Not sure he knows."

"If Mortie spills any other interesting facts, be sure to call me. I'm helping Jack look into the incident. He's writing a story about it for the newspaper."

"Figured. I best git going. See you this weekend, if not before."

I waved at Gertie, then picked up an empty basket and headed to the nursery for the pumpkins. As I loaded the first of ten, I wondered if Jack knew about this discrepancy in the timeline. The longer I thought about it, the more certain I was that this juicy piece of information could change the direction of our investigation significantly.

Picking pumpkins, I realized, was an important task. I knew I would need large, round ones for carving as well as small ones to accent my table display. After finding several tall, thin ones, I decided to do a display for the porch as well. I paid for all my purchases, loaded them into my car, and headed to the newspaper. As promised, Jack was ready and waiting to begin our sleuthing for the day.

"I ran into Gertie," I led off as soon as I entered the building. "Mortie told her that Dru Breland hadn't been entombed in the secret room since the night of Georgia's murder. He indicated Dru had been dead for a shorter time than Georgia."

Jack raised an eyebrow. "Did Mortie know when Dru was murdered?"

"No. He didn't say. If that's true, however, that could mean he did kill Georgia and took off, as everyone assumed, and then was killed at some later date and stashed in the secret room."

Jack crossed his arms and walked to the front of the counter, which was stacked high with this week's edition. "I suppose if that's true, it opens up the suspect pool. I wonder how we can find out for sure when Dru Breland died."

"Savage," we both said at the same time.

Deputy Rick Savage was a nice enough guy. Yes, he could be gruff and surly, but I could tell he had a good heart and genuinely cared for the community he had been tasked to serve and protect. In the past, he'd proven to be reluctant to work with us, although in the end he'd come through. I just hoped this time we could dispense with the formalities and get right down to mystery solving.

I decided to leave my car outside the newspaper and ride with Jack. It didn't make sense to take two cars and I didn't want to drive all over town with a trunk full of pumpkins. The sheriff's office was in the center of town, so Jack parked under a large tree with orange leaves that grew along the street lined with a row of commercial buildings.

"What can I do for the two of you today?" Deputy Savage asked the moment we walked into the reception area of the small office the deputy used for official county business.

"We're here about the body that was found in the secret room on Rhett Crawford's estate," Jack began.

"Figured."

"Mortie told Gertie that Mr. Breland hadn't been dead since the night Georgia Darcy died," I added. "Is that true?"

Deputy Savage looked surprised by my statement. "Mortie told you that? As in the ghost Gertie says lives in her house?"

"One and the same," I confirmed. "Is it true?"

Savage hesitated.

I glanced at Jack, who indicated we should wait for Savage to reply.

"Yes," he eventually said, "it seems to be. Georgia Darcy was found dead in the toolshed five years ago and it appears, based on preliminary reports, Dru Breland has only been dead for about a year."

I looked Savage in the eye. "So Breland could have killed Georgia and taken off, like everyone assumed, and then someone else killed Breland years later."

"That possibility does exist. In fact, the more I think about it, I'm almost certain that's what happened, although we don't yet have conclusive evidence to support the theory that the two victims were killed by different people. All we really know is that they died at different times. Beyond that it's all speculation."

"Did Crawford still own the estate when Breland's body was placed in the room?" Jack asked.

"That's the assumption we're operating under, although that's also inconclusive. We know Crawford sold the house at about the same time Breland died. The two events were close enough in time that it's impossible to determine which came first. It's also important to remember that there's no evidence to support the idea that Breland was killed in the room. The body wasn't found until after the room had been demolished, so it's hard to know for certain. It's been determined that Breland has been dead twelve to fourteen months, but that doesn't necessarily mean his body was placed in the room twelve to fourteen months ago. The body could have been placed there anytime between when he died and when the walls came down six days ago."

This case was becoming more and more interesting.

"Were you the one to investigate Georgia Darcy's murder?" I asked.

"Sheriff Bowman sent over a deputy from the main office to take the lead because it was such a high-profile case, but I assisted."

"I don't suppose you'd mind sharing the name of the deputy who oversaw it?" Jack asked.

"Andrew Hewitt. That's public record. There were quite a few articles in the *Gull Island News* covering the murder and the investigation. You might want to do some research before you bother me with routine questions."

Ouch. Savage was definitely in a cranky mood.

"I'll do that." Jack simply smiled, as if he didn't mind in the least that he'd just been taken down a peg.

"What can you tell us about the initial investigation?" I asked.

"There were twelve people on the estate including Georgia Darcy at the time of the murder: in addition to her, the host and his wife, two employees, and seven guests. The groundskeeper found Ms. Darcy's body in the toolshed at approximately eleven-twenty p.m. He reported it to the host, Rhett Crawford, who called me. I reported the incident to the county office and responded to the call. Everyone except the victim's date, Dru Breland, was interviewed. Some of the guests had specific and verifiable alibis for their whereabouts after the time the victim had last been seen by the group, others didn't. All ten people we spoke to seemed open and willing to share what they knew. After a preliminary investigation, it was determined by both myself and Deputy Hewitt that Dru Breland had most likely killed Ms. Darcy and fled."

"Do you have access to the statements given by those ten people?" I asked.

"Yes, I do."

"Would you mind sharing them with us?"

"Actually, I would. I'm sure Jack here can dig up what he needs for his article from the information provided in the public records. Now, if you'll excuse me, I have a busy morning."

Jack stood and I followed his lead.

"Oh, by the way..." I turned just as I started out the door. "I'm having a dinner party on the thirty-first. It'll be a small affair with a simple menu, but I'd like you to come."

Savage frowned.

"You don't have to let me know right now, but please do think about it. I'm sure we'd all love to have you, and I promise fun will be had by all. I plan to keep it simple and casual. Maybe fondue with a few sides."

"I might have to work that night."

"So come over after. It'll be fun. I promise."

"I'll have to see how things go and let you know," Savage eventually answered.

Well, that was something. I fully expected him to flat-out refuse. Victoria Vance would be home in time for the party, and somehow, I had the feeling Savage knew that. He and Victoria had shared a night of passion that had left love-'em-and-leave-'em Victoria shattered and confused. She'd left the island shortly after that for a business trip to Hawaii and then she'd gone to LA, so as far as I knew, they hadn't yet had an opportunity to discuss the fallout from that night, but after speaking to Savage at the time, I wasn't sure they'd been in communication at all.

"So what's this about a dinner party?" Jack asked.

"I just came up with the idea this morning, but I planned to invite you. It'll be just the writers' retreat gang plus a few others. I'm thinking at around six. Like I said, it'll be casual. I'll fill you in on the details when I figure everything out."

Jack opened the car door for me and I slid in. "Sounds good. So about that date you promised we'd have but somehow seem to be avoiding…"

I groaned.

"I'm thinking tomorrow night might be a good opportunity. We have the writers' retreat meeting on Thursday and the harvest festival starts on Friday and runs through the weekend, which will bring us to Halloween week."

I paused before I answered. Me and my big mouth. Why had I ever agreed to an actual date with Jack? I could sense we were navigating dangerous territory.

"Okay," I finally said after Jack slipped into the driver's side door. "We may as well get it over with. I guess we can go out on a real date tomorrow evening, but keep it casual and don't read too much into it."

"Be still my heart." Jack grinned.

I supposed my acceptance of his invitation had been rather harsh.

"You know I like you," I added. "And we do seem to have fun together. And if I were in a place where I was looking to date, I'd definitely consider dating you. It's just that …"

"You aren't in a place where you want to jump into anything serious," Jack finished for me. "Don't worry. I'll keep it casual. Wear jeans and bring a sweatshirt. It may get chilly before the end of the evening."

I tried not to grimace as I accepted defeat and reconciled myself to the fact that this date was going to happen. "Where exactly are we going?"

Jack winked. "It's a surprise, but don't worry. I'm certain you'll be quite happy with my choice."

Jack's teaser had made me curious. "So, when you say wear jeans, you mean actual jeans? Nothing dressy? Nothing requiring heels?"

"Nothing dressy and nothing requiring heels."

I fought the certainty that this would turn out to be a very bad idea indeed. It had been a long time since I'd been on a date and Jack was about as dateable as any man I'd ever met. "And we'll keep this just between us? No one else needs to know."

"I agreed to that stipulation when I first asked and I'm a man of my word."

"Okay. I guess we can go on a date under this specific set of circumstances."

"Wonderful. Now where should we start with our interviews?"

"Were you able to get hold of all four witnesses who still live on the island?"

Jack nodded. "Yes, and all were happy to speak to us. I didn't set up specific times because I wasn't sure how the day would unfold, but I did tell everyone we'd be by at some point today."

"Then let's start with Olivia Cotton. I seem to remember she owns a bakery and I'm starving."

Chapter 3

Simply Sinful was a full-service bakery with both takeout and eat-in options. When we walked through the front door, the first thing that hit me were the delightful scents of cinnamon, apple, vanilla, pumpkin, and chocolate all melded together to create the perfect aroma. Jack and I took a seat at one of the small white tables surrounded by pretty pink chairs while we waited for Olivia to complete the transaction she was handling.

"Maybe we should have called ahead," I commented as I took in the long line reaching from the counter to the door.

"Yeah. I just realized an afternoon visit would have made more sense for a bakery owner. I guess we can get something to eat and then make an appointment for this afternoon."

I glanced at the glassed-in display case and felt my stomach rumble. Making a choice wasn't going to be an easy task, especially when all four of the daily specials looked like something I'd kill for. Maybe I'd buy extras and take them home to share with my retreat mates. I looked away from the display case as a tall woman with black hair wearing a pink-and-white pantsuit approached.

"My name is Frangelica and I'll be waiting on you. The specials are on the board near the cash register and all the items on the menu are available except the strawberry torte. Can I start you off with something to drink?" she asked after setting menus in front of us.

"Coffee," I answered. "With cream."

"Same here, only black," Jack seconded. "We're actually here to speak to Olivia. Can you let her know Jack Jones is here?"

"I'd be happy to. I'll get those coffees and then be back to take your order. The blueberry scones are to die for and the pumpkin muffins have been popular as well. If you'd prefer a freshly made doughnut, the maple bars have been selling like hotcakes. Look over the menu and let me know if you have any questions."

I watched the waitress walk away. "It all sounds so good."

"While they all sound wonderful, I'm a purist, so I think I'll stick with a glazed doughnut," Jack commented as he considered the menu.

"I have to try the blueberry scone, although the chocolate croissant sounds wonderful too. I think I may get a box of treats to go. I know Clara has a sweet tooth and I've noticed George enjoying a doughnut a time or two. How did I not know about this place?"

"I think it's fairly new. When I called Olivia about the interview she mentioned she'd just reopened a bakery that I guess had been closed for several years after the previous owner passed away."

I looked around the bright, cheery room. "She did a wonderful job with the décor. It's a little pink for my taste, but it has a feeling that's both fresh and nostalgic, and I love these little round tables. I feel like I'm sitting in an outdoor café in Paris."

"Have you ever been to Paris?" Jack asked.

"Several times. It's one of my very favorite cities, along with Rome and Cairo."

"Cairo? Really?" Jack sounded surprised.

"I love the ancient city despite the inherent danger that seems to be lurking around every corner. I'm not saying I'd want to spend a lot of time there, but everyone should visit Egypt at least once if for no other reason than to see the pyramids."

"I haven't been, but I'll have to make a point of going," Jack said. "Before I bought the paper I had an idea of doing a world tour, but now that I'm responsible for a weekly newspaper, I guess I'll have to put those plans on hold."

"How are things going at the paper?" I asked.

"If I had to make a living off it I'd be in trouble, but as mostly a hobby, it's working out just fine. I'm not sure I'll want to do it forever, but for now it feels just right, and I do enjoy the nostalgia of the whole thing."

"That's exactly how I feel about running the resort. When Garrett first asked me to help, I wasn't sure I wanted to, but now that I've settled in and gotten to know so many wonderful people, I feel like I could actually make a home here."

"Do you miss the city?"

"Sometimes. But I feel like I'd miss Gull Island if I left as well. I guess at this point I'm of the mind to focus on building a life here and then wait and see how it all works out."

Jack smiled and nodded to a spot behind my head. "Here comes Olivia with the coffee."

"Jack." Olivia smiled as she set two cups of coffee on the table. "I'm so sorry you had to wait. Did Frangelica take your order?"

"Not yet, but I can see you're busy."

"Wonderfully so. What can I get you? The pumpkin muffins are fresh out of the oven."

"I'll just have a glazed doughnut and I think Jill would like a blueberry scone."

"Yes, that would be great," I confirmed.

"Let me grab those and then we can chat."

I watched as Olivia took two white plates with pink trim from behind the counter and then head toward the kitchen. I hated to bother her with a to-go order just then; maybe I'd come back later, when it wasn't so busy.

"Should we offer to come back?" I asked Jack. "Olivia seems willing to talk now, but I can see she really doesn't have the time."

"Yeah, I was thinking the same thing. We could call Claudia Norris to see if she can meet us this morning. Wylie is out on his boat and won't be back until later this afternoon and Tiffany Pritchett said she'd be available after one."

A woman I'd met at the library a few days before entered the bakery and took her place at the end of the line. That reminded me I still needed to pick up a book I'd placed on hold there. I was reminded, as well, of a bit of news George had shared over breakfast that morning. “Did George happen to mention to you that Georgia Darcy wasn’t the first person to have been murdered on the Crawford estate?”

Jack’s expression registered surprise. “No. Who else was murdered there?”

“Over breakfast this morning, George, who’d begun to research the property the minute our meeting was over last night, told me the estate was owned by a man named Clayton Powell before Rhett Crawford bought it. Powell lived there for more than four decades before being stabbed to death in his own bed by an unknown intruder.”

“They never found out who killed him?”

I shook my head. “As far as the sheriff could tell, all the windows and doors were locked from the inside and hadn’t been tampered with. Additionally, the house hadn’t appeared to be disturbed in any way and there weren’t any unexplained fingerprints found at the scene. According to George, Powell was something of a recluse who didn’t often have visitors. In fact, his body wasn’t discovered until almost a month after his death, when someone from the post office reported to the sheriff’s office that Powell hadn’t been picking up his mail.”

“Wow. That sounds almost like a more interesting mystery than the one we’re investigating.”

“Maybe, but the one we’re investigating is timely and better suited for a newspaper article. Still, it might be fun to have the gang look in to it when we have some free time. The story could make a good novel.”

“It could at that,” Jack agreed.

“I know I’m intrigued.”

“Here we go.” Olivia set plates in front of Jack and me, each holding not only the item we’d ordered but several bite-size samples of other offerings. I was truly in heaven.

“Thank you so much,” I responded. “Everything looks fabulous.”

“It really does,” Jack added. “We can see you’re busy. Jill and I can come back later, after things slow down a bit, if you’d like.”

“That’s very understanding of you, but I could use a break. I’ve been here for hours and my feet are killing me. I’m not sure I know anything that might help you with your article, but feel free to ask anything you feel could be relevant.”

“Okay,” Jack said. He set down his doughnut and took out the small notebook I’d seen him carry on many occasions. “I’ll get right to it so we won’t keep you too long. You were at the Crawford estate on the night Georgia Darcy was murdered serving as cook for the party weekend?”

“Yes, that’s correct. I arrived on Thursday morning and was on the grounds until after I was interviewed by Deputy Hewitt on Saturday night.”

“Had you worked for the Crawfords before?”

Olivia shook her head. “That was my first time working for them. I understood they’d used another woman who ran a catering business out of Charleston in the past, but for some reason she was unavailable and gave them my name.”

“Do you know the name of the woman who referred you?”

Olivia paused. “Hannah Stone. At the time of the party I didn’t know her and I’m not sure where she even got my name, but I was happy for the work. It's tough getting started in the catering industry."

"Yes, I imagine it is." Jack took a sip of his coffee and then continued. "And since the party? Have you stayed in touch with Ms. Stone?"

"Not really. Immediately after I booked the job I called to thank her for the referral. She was pleasant but didn't seem particularly interested in deepening our relationship. As a matter of fact, she indicated she might be leaving the area. I'm not certain whether she ever did."

Jack made a few notes in his little book. "You said you reported for work on Thursday morning?"

"Yes. The out-of-town guests were staying for the four-day weekend and I was to cater the meals for the entire time."

"Do you remember who was there when you arrived?"

"The Mr. and Mrs., of course, as well as Mrs. Crawford's sister, Georgia Darcy, and her date, Dru Breland. They came early to get things ready. Mr. Crawford's friend Jedd Boswell and his date, Honey, came early as well, but they weren't on the grounds when I arrived."

"Do you remember when they showed up?" Jack asked.

"I don't recall. I know both Mr. Boswell and his date were at dinner that night."

Jack jotted down a few more notes. "So who all was at dinner on Thursday?"

"There were six of them: Rhett and Hillary Crawford, Georgia Darcy and Dru Breland, Jedd Boswell and Honey. I can't seem to recall her last name."

"And all six of these people were at the party the night Georgia was murdered?"

"They were, along with Tiffany Flannigan, who was Tiffany Pritchett back then, her date, a man named Reggie Southern, the neighbor, Claudia Norris, and her date, whose name escapes me."

So far, Olivia had confirmed what we already knew. I hoped she'd have something interesting to add before the end of the interview. Jack was a fantastic writer, but as a reporter, I knew it would have been quicker for Jack to just name the guests and have Olivia confirm they were all there. Pacing was a skill I was certain he'd quickly develop.

"Let's focus for a bit on the night Georgia Darcy died," I began. "Can you recall the approximate time she left the gathering?"

Olivia narrowed her gaze, then replied hesitantly. "It was shortly after dinner. I guess around nine-thirty. She'd been fighting with Mr. Breland the entire evening and at one point she stomped off into the night. That was the last time I saw her."

"Were you able to observe the comings and goings of the guests?" I asked.

"Yes. I was in and out, refilling the dessert offerings as well as the coffee and punch. Unlike some of the others, though, I wasn't in the room the entire time, but when I spoke to Tiffany it seemed we shared a similar recollection of the evening."

"Did Mr. Breland go after Ms. Darcy?"

"No. The only person I saw leave to follow her was Mr. Crawford."

I glanced at Jack. He made another note.

"And how long was Mr. Crawford gone?" I continued.

"I guess about an hour. Maybe more. Finally, Mrs. Crawford sent Mr. Boswell to fetch him. Both men came back shortly after that, but Ms. Darcy wasn't with them."

"Did Mrs. Crawford seem concerned when her sister didn't return to the party?"

"It didn't look like it. Just between you and me, I don't think they were getting along. I could definitely sense tension between them."

Again, I glanced at Jack, who continued to jot down notes.

"Other than Mr. Crawford and Mr. Boswell, do you remember anyone else who left the room between the time Ms. Darcy stormed off and Wylie Slater reporting he'd found her body?"

Olivia paused. "It was a couple of hours between the time Ms. Darcy went out and her body was found. Maybe more. I imagine everyone left at one time or another to use the facilities or to get some fresh air. It was warm that evening and I know most of them divided their time between the ballroom and the patio."

I took a sip of my coffee before I asked my next question. "How well do you know Wylie Slater?"

"I know him well now, but I'd just met him back then."

"Mr. Slater was the groundskeeper and lived on the estate year-round, even when the Crawfords weren't in residence. Based on that fact, I'm assuming he knew the layout of the property as well as anyone."

"Yes," Olivia answered, "I'm sure he did."

"Do you have any reason to doubt that Mr. Slater found Georgia Darcy's body when and where he said he did?"

"Why, no. Why would he lie?"

I adjusted my position in my chair and then continued. "Did you think it odd that he found Ms. Darcy's body in the toolshed at eleven-thirty at night during a party?"

Olivia hesitated. She frowned and then answered. "At the time, I didn't think it was strange, but now that you've asked the question, I guess it was sort of odd. I mean, why would Wylie even go out to the toolshed at that hour? He certainly wasn't going to do any work on the grounds at eleven-thirty." Olivia looked at Jack. "Have you spoken to Wylie about this?"

"Not yet," Jack said. "He's out fishing and won't be back until later this afternoon. I have no reason to believe he'd done anything wrong, but it would be very helpful if you would keep this conversation to yourself until after we speak to him."

"Of course, although I can assure you Wylie isn't the sort to hurt anyone. I feel certain there's a logical explanation for why Wylie went to the shed that evening. Maybe he needed supplies, or maybe Mr. Crawford asked him to fetch something he needed."

"As I said, at this point all we want to do is speak to him," Jack reiterated.

Olivia looked toward the line that had gotten even longer while we'd been speaking. "I really should get back. I'm afraid if I don't, the line will end up clear out the door. We can continue this later if you'd like. Things aren't quite as busy in the afternoons."

"Just one more question before you go," I said as Olivia prepared to stand. "In your opinion, based on what you observed, was Georgia Darcy sleeping with her brother-in-law?"

"Absolutely. There isn't a doubt in my mind that they'd been fooling around for quite some time."

Jack and I thanked Olivia and promised to stop by again for a follow-up. I never did order the takeout pastries, but perhaps I'd stop by for those later as well.

"How did you know Rhett and Georgia were having an affair?" Jack asked after we returned to the car.

"I didn't, but I suspected it, so I just tossed it out to see what her reaction would be. One thing I've learned in my years as a reporter is to frame the really important and revealing questions in the form of statements, then look for the reactions."

Jack shook his head. "You're really something. I'm realizing I can learn a lot from you when it comes to the interview process."

"And I know you have a lot you can teach me about framing a novel."

"I'm happy to, anytime you'd like. So, on to Claudia Norris?"

I nodded. "Sounds good to me."

"I wonder if Claudia lived next door to the estate when Powell lived there," Jack mused.

I shrugged. "If you're really interested we can ask, but remember, we don't want to get distracted by a new mystery until after we bring this story home."

Chapter 4

Claudia Norris lived in a beautiful home perched right on the sand of a wide beach. The surrounding grounds were fantastic, but I wondered if it didn't get lonely, living by herself in a huge house bordered by acres of land that effectively separated her from the neighbors on either side. Jack had done some research and discovered that at one time Claudia had lived with her younger sister, Madison, who seemed to have moved from the island when they'd had a falling-out over their grandmother's inheritance. I didn't suppose that argument had any relevance to the case, so I didn't plan to ask her about it, but I had to admit to being curious. I'd recently discovered I had a half brother but had spent most of my life as an only child. I couldn't imagine having a sister and not spending time with her.

Jack and I had discussed the interview during our trip out to the estate, deciding that I'd ask the questions and Jack would take the notes, although he was welcome to jump in with his own questions at any time. We'd called ahead, so Claudia, a tall woman with dark hair, was waiting for us when we arrived. She answered the door at the first knock, then showed us out to the patio and pool area, where she had mint iced tea waiting.

"Thank you for agreeing to speak to us," I began after we'd taken our seats. Claudia, who I suspected was in her midforties, wore perfectly pressed slacks, a dressy blouse, and designer shoes with a sensible heel.

"It's not a problem," Claudia assured me. "There wasn't a person on earth more surprised than me to find out Dru had been buried in a secret room all this time. I was certain he'd been guilty of murdering Georgia."

Jack and I had decided not to reveal that Dru had only been dead for a year to anyone at this point in the investigation. We felt it would be beneficial to get a feel for everyone's thoughts when they believed Dru most likely hadn't killed Georgia. If we felt it necessary, we could reveal the timeline when we were further along in the interviews.

"Living next door to the Crawfords, I imagine you knew them fairly well?" I began.

Claudia shook her perfectly coiffed head. "Not really. They lived in Los Angeles and only visited Gull Island a couple of times a year. They seemed nice enough and I did make a point of saying hi when I ran into them in town, but I wouldn't say we were friends. I'm not even sure why they invited me to their party, although I suspect it was Georgia who suggested it."

"Georgia?"

"She spent more time on the estate than either of the Crawfords. She came with Rhett whenever his wife didn't accompany him and came on her own with friends at least a couple of times a year. She was a lot more outgoing than either Rhett or Hillary and would always make a point of inviting me to lunch when she was here. I won't go so far as to say we had a lot in common, but she was funny and easygoing, even a bit outrageous, and I enjoyed spending time with her."

"Were you aware that Rhett and Georgia were having an affair?"

Claudia's deep blue eyes locked with mine. "It was pretty obvious. Whenever the two of them were here without Hillary, they made no secret of their attraction for each other. Not that they were physically intimate when others were around, but when they thought it was just the two of them, they were very demonstrative, and they weren't afraid to walk down my part of the beach hand in hand. Of course, Georgia had a lot of men. She was a very sexual person who wasn't committed to any one man."

I took a sip of my tea before I asked, "Do you think Hillary Crawford knew her sister and husband were sleeping together?"

Claudia was quiet for a moment. "I'm not sure. Rhett appeared to be very devoted to Hillary when she was here, and when Georgia visited at the same time as her sister, she always brought a date. It wouldn't surprise me if Hillary did know what was going on, but it wouldn't surprise me if she didn't either."

"Who else knew of the affair?"

"Wylie for sure and Jedd. Jedd came to the island with Rhett from time to time when Georgia was here and Hillary wasn't. Other than that, I don't know of anyone for certain."

"Did Rhett and Georgia entertain when they were on the island together?"

She shook her head. "They mostly kept to themselves. It's entirely possible Wylie and Jedd and myself, of course, were the only ones who knew of the affair."

"Olivia Cotton knew," I informed Claudia.

"Yes, but not until after Georgia's death. I'm the one who told her, during a conversation over martinis one evening, but she had no idea before that."

I sat forward just a bit. "Assuming Dru Breland didn't kill Georgia, who do you think did? Keeping in mind not only motive but opportunity as well."

Claudia twisted her lips as she considered the question. "I've actually gone over this in my mind many times since I heard they found Dru's body in a secret room. I won't say I was keeping tabs on everyone, and we were all in and out the entire night. It was a warm evening, which lent itself to strolls in the garden and conversations on the patio. Given the fact that there was a good two hours between the time Georgia stormed out and Wylie came in to tell us he'd found her body in the toolshed, I'd say anyone could have done it if all that was considered was opportunity. We don't know where Georgia went after she left or when she was killed. However, assuming Dru didn't do it—and I still think he could have, despite the fact that he ended up dead as well—I'd have to say Rhett or Hillary would be my main suspects."

"Why them?" I asked.

"It occurred to me that either Hillary found out about the affair and hit her sister over the head in a fit of rage or Georgia threatened to tell her sister about the affair and Rhett killed her to save his marriage."

"Why do you think Rhett would even want to save his marriage? It doesn't sound like he valued it much."

"Oh, he valued it. They both did. Rhett and Hillary had gained the recognition and popularity they enjoyed by being a Hollywood fairy-tale couple. They were both beautiful and talented and seemed to be so in to each other. Everyone wanted to be them. People began to follow their every move. Separately, it's doubtful either would have risen to the top."

Interesting. If what Claudia said was true, it seemed Hillary wouldn't have divorced Rhett even if he was unfaithful—yet they *had* divorced. The why behind that divorce might be worth exploring further. It also occurred to me that neither party would want Rhett's infidelity to make the news if the secret to their success was really their status as a fairy-tale couple. That would give both of them an additional motive if Georgia had threatened to go public with her love affair. I should call Alex before he spoke to Hillary. Maybe he needed to work the subject of her ex-husband's infidelity into the conversation.

"Other than Dru, Rhett, and Hillary, can you think of anyone at the party who would have wanted Georgia dead?" Jack asked.

Claudia pursed her lips and narrowed her gaze as she tapped the fingers of her right hand against her left arm. "If I had to name someone other than the ones mixed up in the affair, I'd have to say Jedd Boswell. I don't know it for a fact, but I did notice him watching Georgia throughout the course of the weekend. As I said before, she was a very sexual person who tended to dress rather skimpily. I wouldn't be at all surprised if she'd attracted Jedd's attention. For all I know, she might have slept with him during other visits to the island."

Jack glanced at me. I shook my head. I knew he wanted to ask Claudia about the former owner of the property and his death, but we needed to stay focused.

"Okay," Jack said, closing his notebook. "I guess that's all for now. Thank you for taking the time to meet with us."

"I'm happy to help if I can. I do wonder if Dru was killed by the same person who killed Georgia. Do you know if Sheriff Bowman has an opinion on that? It seems to me the suspect pool would be a bit different if the question was who killed both Dru and Georgia, rather than simply who killed Georgia."

"I'm not sure what the sheriff believes at this point," Jack answered. "But why do you think the suspects would be different for a double homicide?"

"While I don't know Rhett well, he didn't strike me as a man who would kill his own brother."

"What?" I said. "Wait—Dru was Rhett's brother?"

"Yes. I assumed you knew that."

"But they had different last names."

"Crawford is Rhett's stage name. So is Rhett, for that matter. I think I remember hearing his real name is Sam Breland."

I glanced at Jack.

"So Hillary's sister and Rhett's brother were at the party together?" Jack verified.

"Yes, they were. They didn't seem to be getting along all that well, but they were together in theory. I'm honestly not sure if they were seeing each other prior to that weekend. It never came up. What I do know is that the fact they were together seemed to be causing a lot of tension between all the major players."

"Had Dru and Georgia been to the estate together before that weekend?" I asked.

"Perhaps. I'm not privy to all the comings and goings at the estate. I tend to keep to myself, and I find that at most times visitors to the Crawford property tended to keep to themselves as well. I will say that if they had been together in the past I don't think either Rhett or Hillary were aware of it. Rhett seemed genuinely upset that his brother and his mistress were an item."

This mystery seemed to be getting more and more convoluted.

"So what now?" I asked Jack when we returned to the car.

Jack looked at his watch. "It's almost one and Tiffany said she'd be available after that, although I feel I need to try to sort everything out in my mind before we speak to her."

"Let's head back to my place. We can make some notes on a whiteboard. I find having visuals really helps."

"That sounds like a good idea. Maybe George will be around and can fill us in on the results of his research while we're there. I think a global approach might be best."

"Let's stop by the paper first so I can get my car. It's full of pumpkins and fall decorations. I should take them inside."

"You can drop your car off there and ride along with me on our afternoon interviews and I'll bring you back to the resort when we're done for the day."

"You should plan to stay for dinner. I'm just going to barbecue a London broil and maybe make a salad."

"Sounds perfect."

We found George and Clara sitting on the back deck enjoying a sandwich when we arrived. Blackbeard was watching from his perch and Agatha was curled up in a nearby chair.

"I was wondering where you'd gone off to," George said as soon as we walked onto the deck.

"We've started the interview process," I told them. "So far, we've met with Olivia Cotton, the cook for the weekend, and Claudia Norris, the next-door neighbor."

"Learn anything interesting?"

"Almost too much. We decided we'd get what we have on a whiteboard before we continue. We'd welcome some feedback if you have time."

"Got nothing but time. What do you have?"

Jack went inside and grabbed a blank whiteboard from the stack. He brought it out onto the deck and I revealed the information we'd gleamed during the morning interviews while Jack wrote everything down. By the time we'd finished we had a confusing web of links and arrows connecting the five people we considered to be the major players.

"Secret kisses, secret kisses," Blackbeard repeated the same thing he'd parroted the previous evening.

"Lots of secret kisses as far as I can tell," I replied.

"Okay, so Rhett was sleeping with his wife's sister and his mistress was dating his brother," George began.

"Oh, this is juicy." Clara clapped her hands.

"Additionally, Rhett's best friend may have had a thing for his mistress and Rhett's wife may have known her sister and husband had quite the thing going on, supposedly behind her back," George added.

"Exactly."

"Sounds like a soap opera," Clara said. "How fun. Now we just need an illegitimate child to round things out."

An illegitimate child? Now that *would* add a twist. What if Georgia was pregnant with Rhett's baby and decided to go public with the affair? I doubted that was the case, though I made a mental note to check out Georgia's physical state with Savage just the same.

"There's one additional piece of information you don't have," I said to George and Clara. "Mortie told Gertie that Dru hadn't been dead since the night of the party. Savage confirmed that he'd only been dead about a year and wasn't certain if he'd been entombed in the secret room for the entire time."

"So Dru could have killed Georgia," George commented.

"Yes, he could have," I confirmed. "It's very possible that he killed Georgia and then took off, just as everyone suspected at the time, but then someone caught up with him, killed him, and stashed him in the secret room."

George leaned forward, crossing his arms on the table in front of him. "That really might change things."

"Right now, we're keeping this point to ourselves. Savage knows, and Mortie and Gertie know, but other than that we plan to keep it to our group."

"If Gertie knows Dru didn't die the night Georgia did, everyone will know before the end of the day," George said mildly.

He had a point. Perhaps I should call her.

"Were you able to dig up anything significant about the estate other than that the owner before Crawford was murdered in his bed?" Jack asked.

"Jilli told you that, did she?"

"She did. I find that very interesting and want to discuss it with you in more detail, but not while I'm working on the story about the body in the secret room. Have you found out any more about that?"

"Not a lot so far. I did learn the room wasn't part of the original structure. I don't know how much later it was added; I just know it wasn't on the original blueprints. Apparently, though, the original architect designed the property to include an underground passage from the main house to the atrium."

"Atrium?" I asked.

"That's a separate building the original owner built for his gardening hobby, but it hadn't been used in years. Rhett Crawford had it torn down when he bought the property. I'm not sure if that's relevant, but you never know what little piece of information might prove to be important later down the road."

"Did he build another structure where the atrium stood?" I asked.

"No. I believe the area was covered with lawn."

"And the underground passage?"

"I suppose it was blocked off. I'm not entirely certain yet."

"Secret room, hidden passages. Seems like this has all the makings of a horror flick," Jack said.

"I guess it does, although I'm not sure how either played into the murder after the dinner party."

"Speaking of dinner parties," I said. "I know this is totally off topic, but I'm planning a casual dinner party for the writers' retreat gang and a few others on the thirty-first. I hope you'll both attend."

"Of course," George answered. "It sounds like a nice idea."

"The spirits will be out and about," Clara added.

"If they are, they can come too, as long as they don't eat too much."

"I don't think they'll eat anything at all," Clara responded in a quite serious tone of voice.

"Great; then we have a plan." I smiled. "I'll call Victoria and Alex to let them know. They should both be back by then. If you see Brit, let her know as well. I've already invited Gertie and Deputy Savage. Which reminds me: I have pumpkins in the car, if anyone wants to help me unload them when we're done here."

"I think we are, unless anyone has any other input," Jack said.

"I have a few ideas, but I'd like to noodle on them a bit before I discuss them," George said.

I glanced at Clara, who appeared to be deep in thought. "I'm sensing there may be another death to consider," she said at last.

"Another death?" I asked. "In addition to Dru Breland and Georgia Darcy?"

"Yes. My reading last night was less than conclusive, but I did sense there may be a third victim involved. Someone who hasn't yet been considered."

"Who?" I wondered.

Clara frowned. "I'm not sure."

I glanced at Jack, who looked as puzzled as I felt. "Everyone else who attended the party is still alive," I said to Clara. "Do you think you might be picking up on the death of the man who owned the estate before Rhett Crawford?"

"No." Clara shook her head. "This death is related to the others. I can't see how quite yet, but I sense an energy with unresolved issues. Perhaps there was another person we haven't yet identified."

"Everyone seems to agree there were just the twelve people on the property the night Georgia was killed," I argued.

"Yes. Well, I guess we'll see."

"Okay. If you figure it out, let us know. In the meantime, we can do some research to see if there were other murders or unexplained deaths on the island around the same time. Maybe the death you're sensing didn't occur on the estate."

"Perhaps," Clara answered. She narrowed her gaze and stared off into space, as if looking at something only she could see.

"So what do you think about Clara's third victim?" Jack asked as we walked out to my car to begin unloading the things I'd purchased that morning.

"I'm not sure. I've known Clara's insights to be right on target, but I've also noticed her tendency to skew things when strong emotions are involved. So far, I haven't seen an emotional distraction with this case. If there was a third victim—and I'm not saying there was—the identity could provide an important clue. At this point I think we should keep an open mind and see where our investigation takes us."

Jack opened the back door and lifted out a large pumpkin. "Where do you want this?"

"Just set all the big pumpkins on the porch. I'll arrange them later. Everything in bags and the small pumpkins can go on the dining table."

"It looks like you have a lot of stuff here."

"I'm excited about the holiday and I guess I went a little overboard. I've never really been one of those people who likes to *do* the holidays, but this year I find I'm very excited to embrace it all."

Jack and I set the pumpkins we were carrying on the porch and were returning to the car for the next load when his phone rang. He glanced at the caller ID, then said he needed to take it. He walked slightly away from me before answering, indicating that the conversation was one he didn't want to have overheard.

I grabbed several of the bags from the car and headed into the house to give him additional privacy. Several minutes later, he followed me inside, carrying more bags. I couldn't help but notice the scowl on his face.

"Is everything okay?" I asked.

Jack set the bags on the table. "Yeah. Everything's fine. It was just my agent. She's been putting pressure on me to sell the paper and return to writing full-time. I've told her a million times that I'm enjoying my life here on Gull Island and the break from writing novels has been good for me, but I think she's afraid I'll disappear into obscurity if I don't continue to pump out a new release on a regular schedule."

"Seems unlikely," I supplied. "You're a huge name. You don't need a new release for people to remember who you are. Besides, it hasn't been a year since your last book."

"And she still wants me to do a talk show next week. I pointed out that next week was ridiculously short notice, but one of the guests they had lined up had to cancel at the last minute and they need someone to fill in. She thought it was a good opportunity to start promoting the next book."

"Are you going to do it?"

"I don't know. I don't want to, but I don't want my agent to have a total meltdown."

"Sounds like you need a new agent."

Jack laughed. "If only that were possible. The problem is that my agent is also my mother."

"Your mother?" I gasped. "How did that happen?"

"I was in college when I wrote my first book. Mom stepped in to handle things, and at the time I was glad to have her do it. But now…"

"Now you want a bit of separation but don't know how to achieve that without destroying your relationship with the person who raised you."

"Exactly."

Chapter 5

Later that afternoon, Jack and I went to pay a visit to Tiffany Flannigan, who was Tiffany Pritchett at the time of Georgia's death. Hillary Crawford was a rich, beautiful, famous, and entitled actress from Hollywood, so I had a hard time figuring out exactly how she'd become friends with a sweet, timid, hometown girl like Tiffany. Still, the information we had indicated that the two women had indeed been close, which was the reason Tiffany had been at the party that weekend.

Tiffany had two young children and didn't want to have to get a sitter, so we agreed to meet her at her home. Like Claudia, she was expecting us and had set a pitcher of lemonade and glasses on a table on her back deck. Her daughter, who was three, played quietly on the lawn near where we were sitting and her one-year-old son napped peacefully in his stroller, which was nearby in the shade.

"You have a lovely home," I said to the short brunette with a sunny smile after we'd all settled around the table.

"Thank you. Vince and I have been working hard to make it livable. We couldn't afford a lot when we bought the place, so we had to settle for a fixer-upper, but now that we've had the opportunity to add our own special touches, I think it's just about perfect for our little family at this stage in our lives."

"This neighborhood is actually increasing in value," Jack commented. "I did an article on this and a few other neighborhoods a few months back, focusing on areas that had sunk into disrepair but were being revitalized by young couples such as yourselves, who were attracted by the affordable housing."

"I saw that article and I agree with your assessment. Quite a few of the older, run-down homes have sold to young families in the four years we've been here. They're even putting in a new park down the street."

"I saw that when we drove by," I said. "I'm sure you'll get a lot of use out of it."

"I know we will, and it will help to improve property values as well. Vince and I hope to be able to afford to move into a larger home in a few years, which will only be possible if we can get a good price for this one."

"Are you thinking of having more children?" I wondered.

"Vince wants five."

Five? Yikes.

I decided the chitchat portion of our visit had run its course and steered the conversation to what we were there to discuss. "I'm sure as a young mother you have a busy schedule, so I want to say up front how grateful Jack and I are that you took the time to meet with us."

"No problem. I'm not sure I know anything that would help you with your story, but I'm happy to help in any way I can. What would you like to know?"

Jack started off by asking what she knew about the eleven other people on the property the night Georgia died. Just as the others we'd spoken to had, she reported that Dru and Georgia had been fighting, which led to her slapping him and taking off into the night. She also told us Rhett had gone after her and, when he hadn't returned after an hour or so, Hillary had sent Jedd out to look for him. So far, her story was lining up with what we already knew. The thing was, what we really needed was something we didn't know.

Finally, I asked the question that had been playing in the back of my mind. "How exactly did you and Hillary become friends?"

"When I first met her, I had no idea who she was. I know that must sound crazy because everyone in America knows who Hillary Crawford is, but I'd just recently graduated college and during that time I went to school and worked and didn't see any movies or even own a television. Anyway, Hillary was walking on the beach in front of her estate. It was late afternoon in the late fall and there wasn't anyone else around. I'd been at a friends' who lives to the north of Gull Island and was on my way home in my little fourteen-foot fishing boat with an outboard motor. I was alone in this tiny boat and could see that a storm was rolling in, so I was staying close to the shoreline. I was passing the Crawfords' property when I saw

Hillary trip over something and fall to her knees. I cut my engine and called out to her, asking if she was okay. She called back to me that her ankle really hurt and she was afraid she may have broken it. I pulled my boat up onto the shore and went to see if I could help her. Luckily, I had my phone and called for help. Hillary was in a lot of pain, so I tried to keep her distracted while we waited for the paramedics by telling her funny stories about myself. I'm a bit of a klutz and had had plenty of my own stumble and falls, plus I can be socially awkward, so I have an arsenal of embarrassing moments to talk about."

Tiffany took a deep breath before she continued. "Anyway, the paramedics showed up and I went on my way. I told a neighbor what happened, and she's the one who filled me in on who Hillary Crawford was. I have to admit to being a bit starstruck and embarrassed when I realized who I'd shared the hit parade of my most awful moments with, but a few days later a huge bouquet arrived from Hillary, thanking me and telling me that I was the most genuine and interesting person she'd met in what seemed like decades. She invited me to come for lunch, I went, and we've been friends ever since."

I grinned. "What a great story. Do you still stay in touch?"

"We do. I don't see her often—maybe once every seven or eight months—but we email and text and generally stay up on the goings-on in each other's lives. She calls me her reality barometer."

"Reality barometer?" I asked.

"She's surrounded by people who worship and adore her but don't really know her. At least not the real her. Given the way our relationship started off, with me airing all my embarrassing stories to a total stranger, she knows I can be real, even with her. If she starts to get caught up in her own hype, she calls me and we talk about ordinary things like doing laundry and breastfeeding."

I laughed. "I love it. Everyone needs a friend like you."

Tiffany just smiled.

"I need to ask some specific questions about the night Georgia died," I continued. "I realize some of these questions may hit a nerve and I apologize for that in advance, but Jack and I are trying to unravel what seems like a fairly tangled mystery."

"That's fine. You can ask whatever you like."

"Okay, great. Let's start off with a sensitive one. From what we've learned, Rhett was having an affair with Georgia before the party. Did Hillary know that was going on?"

"No," Tiffany answered. "Not until that weekend. Hillary suspected Rhett was being unfaithful, but she didn't know with whom. She thought it might be an actress he worked with frequently and shared with me that her relationship with Rhett had become all about the image it presented and the boost it had given to their careers. Rhett would treat Hillary like a princess when there were other people around but then totally ignore her when they were alone. I found the idea that she was staying in a relationship with a man she knew was cheating on her to be completely unimaginable, but she said she'd never loved Rhett and didn't really care what he did when they weren't together."

"So how did she find out that the person he was sleeping with was her sister?" I asked.

"Georgia had come to the party with Rhett's brother, Dru, and she seemed to be going out of her way to make it known on the first day that she and Dru were most definitely sleeping together. The fact that Dru and Georgia had become intimate didn't bother Hillary, but it seemed to make Rhett nuts. That confused Hillary at first because she couldn't imagine why Rhett would care who his brother slept with, but then she realized the reason Rhett was so upset about his brother and her sister hooking up was because Georgia had been the one he'd been having the affair with all along."

"Was she mad?"

"Yes, but I think more than mad she was hurt. She wasn't surprised Rhett had been sleeping around, but she was hurt that her little sister would sleep with her husband. Hillary confronted Georgia and they argued. Somehow, Dru found out Georgia had been sleeping with Rhett, and that made him angry as well. By the night of the murder, Hillary and Dru were both angry at Rhett and Georgia, Rhett was angry at Dru and Georgia, and Georgia was angry at Hillary and Dru, but no, before you ask, I don't think Hillary killed anyone. Rhett I'm not sure about. He really did seem to be overly emotional about the situation. And when it looked like Dru had killed Georgia, I wasn't surprised in the least. As far as I'm concerned, it could have been either man."

"Let's assume for a moment that Dru didn't kill Georgia. Would Rhett be your first choice?"

"Part of me thinks it was Rhett, but another part believes he really cared about Georgia. Hillary and I have discussed that night on more than one occasion, and it's Hillary's opinion that her husband might have been a cheater, but he wasn't a killer. In my opinion, if it turns out neither of the brothers killed Georgia, I'd take a look at Wylie Slater."

This was the second time Wylie's name had come up.

"Why do you think it might have been Wylie?"

"First of all, he lived on the property. He would have been around during those times when Georgia was at the estate with Rhett and Hillary wasn't. I'm willing to bet Georgia spent a lot of her time on the property wearing skimpy bikinis and nothing else. Wylie is a young, red-blooded male. I guarantee he noticed. And I can pretty much guarantee Georgia found pleasure in teasing him and leaving him hanging.

"Additionally," Tiffany continued after a brief pause, "he's the one who found Georgia's body. It seemed a little odd to me that he would just stumble across her remains stuffed in the toolshed at eleven-thirty at night, but that's exactly what he told everyone happened."

Tiffany took a deep breath, then released it. "And then there's the fact that Dru's body was recently found in that secret room off the wine cellar. There aren't a lot of people who even knew about that. I didn't know about it. Wylie, however, lived on the property, and for much of the year he was there alone. Plenty of time to snoop around, looking for hidden passages and secret rooms."

"It seems you have a pretty good theory," Jack jumped in.

"Maybe, but I have absolutely no proof. I didn't see or hear anything on the night Georgia died, and I didn't notice anything that would lead me to believe one of the guests had just killed two people. If it's proof you're looking for, I'm afraid you have a tough road ahead."

Tiffany wasn't wrong. Part of the problem with murder mysteries that were five years old or more was that most if not all the physical evidence that had once existed was usually long gone.

"Reggie Southern went to the party as your date," Jack said, redirecting the conversation.

"Yes, that's correct."

"Had you dated long?"

"I guess a couple of months. It was nothing serious, but Reggie was a good guy and we had some fun together. He wasn't the sort to appreciate a party like the ones the Crawfords threw, but Hillary invited me and I wanted to go, so he agreed to attend with me. Our relationship didn't last more than a couple of months after the party, but we remained friends. He's living in Charleston now. I have his address if you want to speak to him."

"Thank you; that would be helpful." Jack smiled. "Do you have any reason to believe Reggie could have been mixed up in whatever happened that night?"

"Reggie? No way. He didn't even know those people. Like I said, he just went there as a favor to me, because I needed a date."

"How about Trent Truitt, Claudia's date?"

"I don't really know him. I'm not sure how Claudia hooked up with him. I'd never seen him before that night and have never seen him since."

"Okay." Jack sat back. "I guess that's about it unless you have something you want to add."

Tiffany hesitated. "There is one thing. It's probably nothing and I'm not sure you can do much to check it out now that the house has been torn down, but one day when I was visiting Hillary there she asked me to go into the library to fetch a sweater she'd left lying over the back of a chair. When I went into the room, I noticed that one of the bookshelves was turned outward on one side. I went to check it out and saw there was some kind of hidden tunnel behind the bookcase. You know, like the kind you see in haunted house movies. I asked Hillary about it and she said the house had all sorts of hidden rooms and passages. That was one of the reasons Rhett wanted to buy the property in the first place. She told me that when they initially decided to look for beachfront property on the East Coast, she wanted to be closer to New York, but then Rhett found this mystery house, and before she knew it, he'd bought it."

"Do you think she knew the location of all the rooms and passages?" I asked.

"She said they were dark, dank, and dusty, and she wasn't even a tiny bit interested in exploring them. I asked her who'd been in the secret passage in the library and she said it must have been Rhett, who wasn't at home while I was there but had been earlier in the day."

I wasn't sure the knowledge that the house had many secret passages and rooms would help us at this point, especially because the house and everything in it was gone, but I did find it interesting. Unlike Hillary, if I had a house with secret passages, I'd have been all over the place, checking out every one of them.

A few minutes later we thanked Tiffany and drove back to the resort. When we arrived, Clara met us at the front door.

"Oh good, you're back," she greeted us. 'It's Blackbeard. I opened the back door to go out onto the deck and he flew out before I could stop him. I've been calling him, but he hasn't come back."

I placed my hand on Clara's shoulders. "It's okay. Blackbeard has gotten out before and he always comes back. How long has he been gone?"

"About an hour."

"Okay, I have a few places we can check. Jack and I will go looking for him. Call my cell if he comes back before we do."

"Okay, but hurry. I sense he's in danger. He wants to come home, but he can't."

I glanced at Jack and prayed this was one of those times Clara's predictions were wrong.

Chapter 6

The first place I thought to look for Blackbeard was Sully's, a local bar my half brother used to take him to before Garrett had his stroke and moved into the nursing home. I'd done my best to fill Garrett's shoes when it came to both Blackbeard and the resort, but I'm afraid spending time in a bar wasn't my thing, so the bird hadn't been by for visits as often as I was certain he'd like.

"Afternoon, Sully," I greeted the pub owner, who was stocking inventory behind the bar.

"Jill, Jack. Can I get you something?"

Jack and I both slid onto barstools. "Actually, we're looking for Blackbeard. He got out about an hour ago. Have you seen him?"

"Yeah, I've seen him. He flew in maybe thirty minutes ago. Landed right here on the counter and began chatting a mile a minute."

"Do you remember what he said?" I asked.

"He started off with a few rounds of 'grogs and wenches,' which, as you know, is his normal song when he comes here, and then segued into a rant about 'killing the cat' and 'secret kisses.' Oh, and there was something about 'London Bridge' and 'Humpty Dumpty.' Have you been teaching him nursery rhymes?"

"No, but Clara might have. She seems to have a fascination with them and their history and meaning, which can be dark and at times sort of gross. I mean, have you ever thought of the literal meaning of rhymes like 'Humpty Dumpty'? Basically, he falls off a wall and gets smashed into a million little pieces. It's pretty morbid."

Sully set a couple of glasses of water in front of us. "Yeah, I guess that is a bit dark, but Blackbeard seemed really in to it."

"Did he recite any other nursery rhymes?" I asked. Both "Humpty Dumpty" and "London Bridge" had to do with falling down and being destroyed. Knowing Blackbeard, there could be a clue there.

"Not that I remember. I was busy, so I gave him a treat and sent him on his way."

"Do you know where he might have gone?"

Sully twisted his lips to the side as he thought about it. "He said something about turtle power, so you might check with either Meg or Digger."

"Thanks. I'll check with them. If he comes back by here, call me. I know he's a smart, independent bird, but I worry about him when he's out and about on his own."

Jack and I finished our water and then went back to his car. We slid inside and he placed the key in the ignition. "Where to?" Jack asked.

"Meg is closer, although I suppose it's more likely Blackbeard would seek out Digger. Let's head to the museum first and then swing by the cemetery."

Meg Collins not only ran the local museum but was the woman who organized the local turtle rescue squad. Every year, sea turtles returned to the shores of Gull Island to lay their eggs, and every year, Meg and her volunteers made sure as many of those eggs hatched and made their way to the sea as possible. Digger was both the caretaker for the local cemetery and Meg's staunchest volunteer. Blackbeard used words he'd picked up from television and listening to those around him. He especially liked cartoons and pirate movies and often used phrases found in the dialogue of his favorite shows. *Teenage Mutant Ninja Turtles* was one of them, and both Meg and Digger often wore their turtle team hats, which had a turtle on the top. My guess was if he was repeating "turtle power," he was referring to one of them.

The museum had been built on a hill, which provided an unobstructed view of the ocean in the distance. Coupled with colorful flower gardens and well-maintained walkways, the grounds were a pleasant place to gaze out at the sea or enjoy a snack on one of the many picnic tables. The trees on the grounds were beginning to change to pretty reds, yellows, and oranges, announcing to visitors that fall was in the air.

"Jack, Jill," greeted a woman in her midsixties with neatly styled hair in a natural silver-gray that almost matched the lightweight blouse she wore atop darker gray slacks. "How nice you stopped by."

"We really can't stay. We're looking for Blackbeard."

"I'm afraid I haven't seen him today. Did the little scamp escape again?"

"Yes, and he mentioned something about turtle power to Sully, so we figured he was either heading to you or Digger."

"You should check with him. He should be mowing today."

"We planned to talk to him next."

"By the way," Meg added as Jack and I turned toward the door, "I need a couple of volunteers to help out with the kiddie carnival this weekend if you're free. The shifts are just two hours and you get a free hot dog."

"I'd be happy to," I offered.

"I'm in as well," Jack seconded.

"Great. If you could show up at the kids' camp at ten-thirty on Saturday that would be fantastic. The shift is from eleven to one, but I'll need to show you what to do. I thought I had it covered, but Wylie Slater and his girlfriend backed out."

That got my attention. "Wylie backed out?"

"This morning. He said he had to go out of town for a few days and wouldn't be back until after the weekend."

"Do you know when he planned to leave the island?"

"I'm pretty sure he's already gone. He said something about picking up his girlfriend and then heading out so they could get ahead of the storm that's supposed to blow in later this evening."

"So he left in his boat?" I clarified.

"That's the way it sounded to me. You seem upset. Is that a problem?"

"No." I shook my head. "I just needed to speak to him about something. It'll keep until he gets back. I guess we'll head over to talk to Digger now. If

Blackbeard is with him, maybe we can catch up with my runaway bird before he takes off again."

We drove to the cemetery directly from the museum. Digger was a nice-enough guy, although I'd found him to be somewhat taciturn in his speech. In the past, he would answer questions readily enough, but it was up to you to keep the conversation going. He had indeed been mowing but, luckily, was taking a break when we got there.

"Afternoon, Digger," I began.

"Afternoon."

"We're looking for Blackbeard. Have you seen him?"

"Yup."

"Is he here now?"

"Nope."

"Has he been gone long?"

"Nope."

I paused and considered my next question. I doubted I'd get a coherent reply, but it was worth a try. "Did he say where he was going?"

Digger raised an eyebrow.

"Did he say anything at all?" I tried again.

"Yup."

"Do you remember what he said?"

Digger frowned. "Nope."

"Did he happen to mention 'Humpty Dumpty' or 'London Bridge'?"

Digger turned his head and spat. "Now that you say it, he *was* yammering on about 'Humpty Dumpty.'"

Okay, now we were getting somewhere. I think.

"Which way did he fly off to?"

Digger pointed.

"Okay, thanks. If he comes back, will you call or text me?"

"Sure. I guess I can do that."

Jack and I returned to his car once again. "Now what?" he asked.

"I'm not sure. Blackbeard isn't one to *yammer on*, despite the way it may sometimes seem. If he's talking about 'Humpty Dumpty' and 'London Bridge,' he has a reason. In both rhymes, something is falling and can't be put back together. I wonder if he's talking about the Crawford house."

"You think he saw it fall?"

"I don't think he was out that day, but he may have been by earlier today and noticed it on the ground, or he may have overheard us talking and gotten the gist of what we were talking about."

Jack looked skeptical. "You think he understands what we're saying when we speak among ourselves?"

"I guess it would be crazy if he did, but since I've been at the resort, if there's one thing I've learned it's that when it comes to Blackbeard, you should expect the unexpected. The Crawford property isn't all that far out of our way. Let's head over there to see what we can find."

Jack shrugged. "Fine with me."

The drive from the cemetery to the land that once made up the Crawford estate but would soon become the Beachcomber Condominium Complex took us about ten minutes. The first thing I noticed was that the entrance was marked with yellow crime scene tape, the second was Blackbeard sitting on top of a pile of rubble. Apparently, once they'd found the body in the secret room they'd stopped working, so the structure hadn't been hauled away yet.

I knew you aren't supposed to cross yellow tape, but my bird was on the other side of it, so not crossing it didn't even enter my mind.

"Blackbeard, where have you been? I've been all over town looking for you."

"'Humpty Dumpty, Humpty Dumpty.'"

"Yes, I know. The house fell down."

"Secret kisses, secret kisses."

"Do you know something about those secret kisses?" I asked. "Is that why you brought us here? To show us a clue?"

Blackbeard flew over to another part of the rubble and landed. If whatever he wanted to show us was now part of the rubble, we'd never be able to figure out what it was.

"The house fell down," I said. "There's nothing to see."

"Secret kisses, secret kisses."

I frowned. Even if Blackbeard had seen Rhett and Georgia kissing, it was very unlikely he'd understood the significance of it, and it had happened five years ago. Could a parrot remember something from that long ago? I wasn't certain, but I doubted it. What if the secret kisses referred to a more recent event? The estate had been abandoned for years, but it was possible someone was on the property exchanging secret kisses as recently as a couple of weeks ago.

"Who did you see kissing?" I tried. Blackbeard wasn't usually able to come up with proper names, though he did seem to have a way of communicating what he'd seen.

Blackbeard just looked at me. I could see I wasn't going to get anything out of him, so I slowly made my way through the rubble. I needed to grab him before he flew off again. Fortunately, I'd thought to bring his tether. When I arrived at the spot where he was waiting, he hopped away. Not far—only about five feet—but far enough that I couldn't reach him to tie the tether to his leg.

"Come on, Blackbeard. I'm tired. It's getting late. We need to get home and make dinner."

"Captain Jack, Captain Jack."

"Yes, Captain Jack is coming for dinner. So how about it, buddy? Will you come along peacefully?"

Blackbeard continued to sit where he was. I glanced at Jack. "Maybe you'll have better luck."

He shrugged and started forward, walking slowly so as not to trip on the debris. When he arrived at the spot where Blackbeard was waiting, he suddenly stopped and looked down.

"Grab him," I instructed.

"I see something beneath the rubble."

"Something important?"

"I'm not sure." Jack bent down and began picking up and setting aside bricks and pieces of wood. "It's a key."

"What kind of key? A house key, maybe?"

Jack held up a small key. It looked more like the kind you'd use for a safety deposit box or perhaps a trunk or even a small personal safe.

"What do you think it goes to?" I asked.

Jack looked around. "I have no idea. I wonder if there's more hidden under this rubble than we first imagined. If Crawford had a secret room, maybe he had a secret safe."

"Rhett Crawford isn't the one who's dead," I pointed out. "He's very much alive and he sold the property knowing it would be torn down. Don't you think he would clean out a secret safe if he had one?"

"Good point. Still, I wouldn't mind looking around."

"The sun is about to set and we don't have flashlights. Let's come back tomorrow. For now, let's grab Blackbeard and go back to the resort." I looked off into the distance. There were heavy black clouds coming in our direction. It looked like we were definitely in for the storm Meg had mentioned. If we were lucky, the rain would hold off until after we grilled the meat.

We weren't.

******

"This is really good," Brit complimented later that evening as we shared the food we'd cooked on the stove. "I'm so glad I waited for you instead of having the peanut butter and jelly sandwich I had planned."

I'd been looking forward to barbecuing, but sitting in front of the fire with George, Brit, Clara, and Jack eating steak and beans and watching it pour outside the large picture window was just about perfect. The fact that Blackbeard was sitting contentedly on his perch and Agatha was curled up in the chair made it even better.

"Did you ever get hold of Victoria?" George asked.

"I did, and she's going to try to contact Rhett and Jedd, but she wasn't sure how successful she'd be. They're both rich and popular enough that there are a lot of people between them and anyone who'd like an audience with them. Still, Vikki is pretty persuasive. My money is on her."

"And Alex?"

"I haven't heard from him. I'll call and bug him tomorrow. I'd hoped we could speak to Wylie then, but it appears he's flown the coop. It does seem more and more likely he could be the killer."

"I know there seems to be evidence lining up against him, but I actually kind of know the chap," George volunteered. "I'd be very surprised if it ends up that he's the guilty party. It's important to keep an open mind."

"How do you know him?" I asked.

"He owns and operates a fishing charter and I've been out with him a few times."

"He bought the boat after the murder on the Crawford estate," I stated.

"Yes. Shortly after."

I frowned. "He worked for the Crawfords as a groundskeeper. I wonder where he got the money to buy a fishing boat a few months after his job for them ended."

"You're thinking maybe Rhett gave him the money as some sort of a bribe to get him to keep what he knew to himself." Brit's eyes lit up as she spoke.

"Maybe. If Dru killed Georgia and Rhett helped him get away, as we suspect, maybe Rhett asked Wylie to move the body into the toolshed and then come into the house at a specified time to tell everyone he'd found her. That would give Dru time to get away and would also deflect suspicion from Rhett because he would have been back at the house well before the body was 'discovered.'"

"What about Jedd?" Jack asked. "Hillary sent Jedd to find Rhett and they came back together."

"Maybe Wylie had already taken care of things before Jedd showed up, or maybe as Rhett's best friend, he went along with the plan. I know this isn't the only possibility, but it's an explanation for how Wylie was able to afford the boat."

"He also could have saved the money," George pointed out. "I imagine he made a good salary working for Rhett Crawford, and he did live on the property rent free. It would be easy to stash away enough money to afford a down payment on a boat."

"True." I looked at Brit. "Did you have any luck tracking down Honey Golden?"

"Yes and no. I found an old Facebook account she no longer uses. In fact, the last post was made four years ago. I used it to find her Twitter account, but she hadn't used that in over a year. I couldn't find any evidence that she had a Snapchat or Instagram account, at least not in her name. As far as I can tell, she was living in Boston when she last used her Twitter account. The trail is cold after that, but I'll keep looking."

"She may not be all that important as a witness anyway. She came to the party as Jedd's date. It's unlikely she was involved in the love triangle or even had an opinion about it one way or another. Still, thanks for looking." I turned back to George. "I found out something that might be of interest to you. It seems the entire house was filled with secret rooms and hidden passages. Tiffany told me the reason Rhett bought that specific property was because of all the hidden rooms and passages."

"It's a shame the house was torn down. I would have loved to have had the chance to explore it a bit."

"Yeah, me too. It sounds sort of spooky and mysterious."

"I wonder why he sold the property," Brit mused. "It seems if it was that awesome, he would have kept it."

"And why to a developer who was just going to tear it down?" Jack added.

"Secret kisses, secret kisses," Blackbeard said.

"Yes, we know about the secret kisses. It seems everyone did, so I'm not sure he'd need to sell the house to cover up an affair. It must be something else."

"Maybe he needed the money," Britt suggested.

"No," Jack countered. "I've looked in to his finances and he appears to be loaded."

"I suppose the house may simply have held too many bad memories," Clara said, speaking for the first time that evening.

"Clara's right," I added. "It sounds like he actually cared about Georgia. Maybe he didn't want a reminder of what happened. It does sound like a tragedy."

"Love and tragedy often go hand in hand," Clara said softly.

I glanced in her direction but, once again, she was looking off into space at something only she could see.

Chapter 7

Wednesday, October 25

Jack and I headed back to the Crawford estate, or at least what was left of it, the first thing the next morning. We weren't sure how long the sheriff's office planned to hold off the developer from continuing with the project. After a bit of discussion, we decided to bring Blackbeard with us and allow him to explore without his tether. It was a risk, I knew, but he seemed to have a handle on exactly what we were looking for, and Jack and I agreed that at this point we were pretty clueless.

"Okay, buddy, here's the deal," I said to my feathered friend as I prepared to release him from his carrier. "We need your help and you seem to know what you're looking for, so we're going to give you free rein. But no flying off. Do you understand?"

"Who's a good bird, who's a good bird?"

"That's right; I need Blackbeard to be a good bird. I already spent half the day yesterday chasing you around town and I wouldn't like a repeat performance today. If you're a good bird, I'll give you a treat when we're done here. Deal?"

Blackbeard tilted his head, as if he were listening to what I was saying, but didn't reply.

"Now, I need you to find whatever it was you were trying to show us yesterday. We're trying to figure out who killed Georgia Darcy five years ago and then Dru Breland four years later."

"Secret kisses, secret kisses."

"Exactly." I opened the cage and Blackbeard flew out. Luckily, he simply flew over to the rubble left by the demolished house and didn't take off. He landed in the same area where we'd found the key the previous day. Chances were there was more to find.

"I'm surprised you trust the little trickster to behave," Jack commented as we walked to the construction site.

"I don't, but he seems to be our best bet at finding a clue. I've noticed Blackbeard likes to be included. Maybe he'll be a good bird today because we're including him in our investigation."

"Let's hope so. I'd hate to lose another day chasing him around."

When we arrived at the spot where Blackbeard was waiting, we took a minute to get the lay of the land. It looked like the house had been taken down in stages. I hadn't witnessed the demolition itself, but based on the amount of rubble it seemed as if they may have taken the house down a section at a time. There was one section still standing, which represented the bottom floor of a separate wing I assumed might have contained guest rooms or perhaps utility rooms and offices. I'd never been inside the estate before it was torn down, but Jack had pulled a set of blueprints from the county office, so we had a general idea of the layout. Not that the house couldn't have been altered or added on to since the original permit was granted. In fact, there was a good possibility it had.

"Okay," I said to Blackbeard, who was still sitting on the same pile of rubble he had first flown to. "Is this where we should look?"

"'Humpty Dumpty, Humpty Dumpty.'"

"Yes, the house fell down and is very broken," I agreed. I looked at Jack. "Let's start digging around carefully. Who knows what we'll find under all this brick?"

As with any construction site, especially one with so much debris, there were a lot of sharp objects to work around, so we decided it was best to go slowly. Blackbeard seemed content to watch as Jack and I removed one brick at a time, so I assumed we were digging in the correct spot.

After more than thirty minutes, Jack stood up straight and wiped the sweat from his brow. "It's going to be tough to know if we've found whatever it is Blackbeard wants us to when we don't know what we're looking for."

"So far, all I've found are bricks, wood, nails, and plaster." I looked at the bird, who seemed to be watching us intently. "I don't suppose you can give us a clue?"

Blackbeard turned his head from side to side. It almost appeared he was thinking about an answer. After several minutes, he spoke: "Hidden treasure, hidden treasure."

I shrugged. "We'll keep digging."

It took an additional twenty minutes before Jack uncovered a necklace. The chain had been broken, but the stones were still set firmly.

Jack held it up. "It looks like a real sapphire surrounded by real diamonds."

"Hillary Crawford is a wealthy woman. It could belong to her," I reasoned.

"That would make sense." Jack looked back at the rubble. "It could also have belonged to any woman who visited the estate at any time. It's more than likely it isn't even associated with the murder, but it could be a clue, so we should hold on to it." Jack handed it to me and I slipped it into my pocket. "Hang on, I see something else." He bent down and began to clear away a new section of debris. After a few minutes, he came up with a knife.

"It has blood on it," I observed.

"Do we know how Dru died?" Jack asked.

"Savage must, but I don't remember him mentioning it. I'll call him."

Jack continued to work while I made the call. Savage wouldn't be thrilled to hear Jack and I had crossed the yellow tape and were digging through rubble I'm sure he considered to be evidence, but maybe I wouldn't have to tell him. As I waited for the call to connect, I wondered why Sheriff Bowman hadn't sent someone to do exactly what Jack and I were doing. They had, after all, found a body in the wreckage.

"Hey, Deputy Savage, it's Jillian Hanford," I said into the answering machine that had picked up after instructing me to call 911 if this was a genuine emergency. "I was wondering about the cause of death for Dru Breland. It would be fantastic if you could call me back as soon as you get this message. I may have found something that could prove to be important to your case."

I hung up and returned to Jack, who was standing near where he'd found the knife.

"Anything else?" I asked.

"Not yet. There's a lot of debris to move. I'm not sure it will be worth the effort unless we suspect there's something important to find."

I glanced at Blackbeard. He just looked at me. I was about to suggest a cold shower followed by lunch when my phone rang. It was Savage.

"Hey, Savage, are you in your office?" I asked.

"I will be in five minutes."

"Perfect. Jack and I are heading your way. We have something to show you."

I hung up and looked at Jack. "Let's go. I think this is what Blackbeard wanted us to find. If he has other ideas, I'm sure he'll come up with a way to get us here again."

"Yeah, okay." Jack tossed a piece of wood to the side. "Maybe the knife will have prints or something to help us figure this out."

Deputy Savage was working on his computer when we arrived. I figured there was no reason to beat around the bush, so I set the knife on his desk before sitting down next to Jack across the desk from Savage.

"What's this?" he asked.

"A knife Blackbeard found on the Crawford estate."

Savage raised a single brow. "Blackbeard found it?"

"Well, he led us to it. It was in the rubble near the far north corner of what was the main house. I don't know for certain this was the weapon used to kill Dru Breland, but we found it in the vicinity of the secret room."

Savage pulled up a file on his computer. He narrowed his eyes as he studied the screen in front of him. "Dru Breland was stabbed to death. I believe you could be correct about this being the murder weapon. I'll send it to the lab and have it tested for DNA and fingerprints. This is a good find, but you're aware that I realize for you to have found this knife where you did, you would have had to have crossed the crime scene tape."

"Blackbeard crossed it," I explained. "Jack and I went in to get him. I mean, we couldn't just leave him there."

Savage let out a snort, but he didn't call me on it. "Did you find anything else?"

I thought about the necklace but decided to keep that to myself for now. "No, that was all. Once we found the knife we came straight here. There may be more to find, but we didn't take the time to look further."

Savage sat back and crossed his arms. "I'm not happy you crossed the tape, but it might be worth my while to have you show me exactly where you found the knife. There could be other items to find. Given the circumstances, it seems a closer look might be warranted."

"We'll be happy to follow you over there and show you where we found the knife, but I have to ask why no one has been there to go through the rubble before now. A body was found in the structure."

Savage said, "Off the record?"

Jack shrugged. "Sure. Off the record."

"Something's going on. I'm not sure what yet, but Sheriff Bowman specifically told me not to disturb the debris. I've inquired a couple of times about taking a closer look, but he just told me that he'll take care of it and I shouldn't bother myself."

"Seems odd. Do you think he's being bribed or persuaded in some way to turn a blind eye?" I asked.

"Maybe. This isn't the first time I've questioned his decisions in recent months. I guess you heard he's decided not to run for another term. Not that I blame him. The guy's been sheriff for more than twenty years and I can see he's tired and worn out. But something more seems to be going on. I hate to think it's something illegal or unethical, but there have been times when it's certainly looked that way. Of course, I don't have the whole story, so there may be a perfectly logical explanation for everything."

I certainly couldn't think of a logical explanation for why Sheriff Bowman would choose not to search through the rubble at the estate, and I was pretty sure Savage didn't think there was one either. "Will you get in trouble for looking around today?"

Savage stood up. "I don't know, but a bloody knife found at the scene of the crime gives me a good reason to look. Let's go."

He took his own car and Jack, Blackbeard, and I followed in Jack's. It bothered me more than a little that Sheriff Bowman was acting all mysterious. He was getting on in years and that could make him less enthusiastic about getting out there and tackling every case that came his way, but it seemed to me he specifically didn't want Deputy Savage to investigate a murder on his own island. That made it look to me as if he really was being bribed or coerced in some way.

"I'm fairly new to the island and haven't had any interactions with the current sheriff," Jack said. "Do you know anything about him? His politics or track record?"

"Not a thing. I've been here even less time than you have. I can ask Garrett about him when I take Blackbeard for his weekly visit, which I probably should try to do this afternoon."

"I need to head over to the paper after we finish up here; I'll drop you back at your place then. Don't forget, we have a date planned for this evening."

"I won't forget," I grumbled.

Jack parked in the driveway behind Savage at the estate. I wasn't sure the good deputy wanted Blackbeard's help, so I opened a window and left him in the car. It was a moderately cool day and Jack had parked under a large tree, so he'd be fine for a while. If it looked like we were going to be here longer, I'd come back to get him.

"Do you happen to know the timing of the house being sold and the contents being evacuated?" I asked. I wasn't sure this was important, but I had the feeling it was.

"Rhett Crawford sold the estate to the developer fourteen months ago. Shortly after, he hired a moving company to empty the house. The contents were put in storage. And based on the report provided by the medical examiner, Dru Breland has been dead between twelve and fourteen months."

"From what I understand, most people believed Dru had been out of the country since Georgia died," Jack said.

"No one's known where he was since he disappeared five years ago. It seemed like a good bet he was out of the country."

"So maybe he heard Rhett sold the property and the contents were going to be put into storage and he came back to get something he left behind," I speculated. "It does sound like he left the area after Georgia's death without having the opportunity to come back to the house."

Savage paused as he looked down at the rubble. He had an expression of contemplation on his face. "That makes sense. We originally believed Breland killed Georgia in a fit of passion and took off immediately. If he came back to the United States, where an arrest warrant was still pending, he must have had a good reason. Assuming he had something with him the weekend of the party that he considered to be of great value, it stands to reason he might have snuck back into the country to retrieve it."

"If that's true and Dru did kill Georgia, the question remains, who killed Dru?" Jack asked.

"Someone must have known he was here," I suggested. "Maybe Hillary. Or even Rhett? Both could have motive, but it seems like a long shot; neither live here, so they wouldn't have simply run into him. If they knew he was going to be here, though, they certainly have the resources to meet him here. They both most likely knew about the secret room as well."

"What about Wylie?" Jack asked, turning to Savage. "We've discussed the fact that he could be a suspect. Maybe he found out Dru was back and killed him. It's been suggested he might have had a thing for Georgia. Maybe he wasn't in on the cover-up, as we speculated earlier. Maybe he really did just find the body and has been stewing about the murder all these years."

"The timing of his trip does seem opportune," I agreed. "He must have known we'd been talking to people. Maybe he did have something to hide."

"It's doubtful Wylie took off to avoid an interview," Savage joined in. "He's only going to be gone for a few days. He must know this whole thing isn't likely to go away in such a short period of time. Besides, I know Wylie. Have for a while. He doesn't strike me as the sort to carry out or cover up a murder."

"What if he's protecting someone?" I suggested.

"Like who?"

"I don't know," I admitted. "My point was that even nice guys can be persuaded to cover up a murder for the right reason."

Savage didn't respond, instead going back to digging through the rubble. Without a clearly defined goal, the task of looking for a clue in this mess was a daunting one.

"Maybe we should get the bird," Savage said after a bit. "It'll take forever for the three of us to pick through all of this. If there's something more to find maybe he can do it."

I returned to the car and released Blackbeard from his crate. "Okay, big guy. If you have a secret you've been keeping, now would be the time to fill us in."

"'Humpty Dumpty, Humpty Dumpty.'"

"Yes, the house came tumbling down. What we want to know is whether there's something buried under the rubble."

Blackbeard flew to the area where Jack and Savage were waiting. He landed on Savage's shoulder and gave him a kiss. Aw, how sweet. I knew the deputy and Blackbeard had a relationship, and today I realized just how special it was.

"Okay, you ornery bird," Savage said gruffly. "Time to do your thing."

"Man overboard, man overboard."

Blackbeard had been the one to call Savage the day Garrett had his stroke and had said that into the phone. Savage had come running. I wondered now if this frequently parroted saying had come up because Savage was here, reminding Blackbeard of that call, or if he knew something about Dru's death.

"That's right," Savage said. "Man overboard. What do you know about a man going overboard at this house?"

"Secret kisses, secret kisses."

"Blackbeard has been saying that since the beginning," I shared. "At first, I thought he was referring to Rhett and Georgia, but what if Dru met someone here? A female someone."

"Blackbeard saw them kissing and then what?" Savage asked. "They fought and she killed him?"

I shrugged. "I don't know. Maybe."

"I keep coming back to the fact that Dru's body was found in the secret room," Jack commented. "There can't be that many people who knew about it."

"True, though Dru might have," I said. "It's entirely possible Dru brought someone to the estate with him or met someone here. If he knew where the room was, maybe he'd opened it and whoever who killed him took advantage of that. In fact, if our theory that he came back to retrieve something is correct, maybe he hid whatever it was in the secret room in the first place."

"I guess that's possible," Jack said. "What now? Do we keep looking?"

I glanced at Blackbeard. "How about it? Last chance. Is there anything you want to show us? Did you see Dru when he was here? Was someone with him?"

"Jack and Jill, Jack and Jill."

Savage looked at us with a raised brow.

"Jack and I didn't kill Dru, but 'Jack and Jill' could be a clue. Clara has been teaching Blackbeard nursery rhymes. He's been saying 'Humpty Dumpty' and 'London Bridge' quite a bit. I assumed that referred to the house falling, but if he did see a man and a woman here, 'Jack and Jill' could be a clue. They came tumbling down too, after all. It could very well be that Blackbeard saw a woman hit or stab Dru to make him come tumbling down. Now we just have to figure out who the Jill in Blackbeard's story is."

Chapter 8

I first came to Gull Island at my half brother Garrett Hanford's request. He'd inherited Turtle Cove from his mother and had been running it as a family resort. Garrett had the stroke about a year ago, and while he was doing much better, he'd realized he would never be able to run the place again, so he'd asked me if I would be willing to come to the island to oversee the renovations it desperately needed to be sold. I'd agreed but eventually decided to open the resort in small phases as a writers' retreat. Even though Garrett lived at the Gull Island Senior Home and was unable to have Blackbeard live with him, visits were allowed, and I made a point of bringing Blackbeard there once a week.

"Man overboard, man overboard," Blackbeard said as soon as he saw Garrett, who believed he was still saying it to show he knew why he'd moved into the senior home rather than coming home to the resort.

"It's good to see you, Blackbeard," Garrett answered. "Is Jill taking good care of you?"

"Secret kisses, secret kisses."

Garrett grinned. "You don't say. Sounds like a juicy conversation-starter."

"It isn't me who's been indulging in secret kisses," I said. "I guess you heard Dru Breland's body was found in a secret room on the Crawford estate."

"I had heard."

"The gang and I are helping Jack look in to it, and ever since we started investigating, Blackbeard has been saying 'secret kisses.' At first, I thought he might be referring to the secret kisses between Rhett Crawford and Georgia Darcy five years ago, but now we think he might have seen Dru with someone at the estate before he was killed."

"Before he was killed? You mean Dru hasn't been in the secret room this entire time?"

I nodded. "He's only been there about a year, although that's something we're keeping secret. It seems Dru did take off after Georgia died, just as everyone thought, but he came back around the time Crawford sold the property. We're assuming it was to retrieve something he was forced to leave behind when he fled."

"I must say that makes for an interesting mystery. Do you have any leads?"

"Yes and no." I filled Garrett in on what we'd found out so far. "We have no way to know who might have killed Dru," I added. "We aren't even certain he was killed at the estate, although that would seem a good assumption. It doesn't help that Sheriff Bowman doesn't want Deputy Savage to investigate. I don't suppose you have any idea what's up with that?"

“I don’t, although you aren’t the first one to mention Bowman’s suspect decisions as of late. I understand he isn’t running for reelection.”

“That’s what Savage said. He’s getting on in years, so I totally understand that. I just hope there isn’t more behind his decision than age. It would be too bad if he started taking bribes at this stage in his career.”

“I take it that Sheriff Bowman not wanting Savage to investigate isn’t going to stop you?”

“That’s correct. Like I said, the gang and I are all over this mystery. I feel like we have a good theory about what occurred the night Georgia died, but Dru’s death is another thing entirely. I’ve been thinking about…” My comment was interrupted by the ringing of my cell phone. “It’s Alex. Do you mind?”

“Go ahead; take it. I have nothing but time.”

I smiled at Garrett. “Hi, Alex. What’s up?”

“I’m sitting in Hillary Crawford’s living room discussing Georgia’s death and realized you might want to listen in. I’m putting you on speakerphone.”

“Thank you; I would like that. And thank you, Ms. Crawford.”

“Hillary, please. I should get rid of the Crawford name altogether, but I’ve been concerned that would hurt my career.”

“I understand completely. I’m afraid I’m coming in at the middle of your conversation. I hate to be repetitive, so if you could catch me up…”

“Alex has been asking about the night Georgia died. Who was there, what I remember happening, that sort of thing. Basically, it all came down to who I thought killed Georgia, and to be honest, just like everyone, I’ve been assuming it was Dru who did it.”

"And now?" I asked.

"Given the fact that his body was found in one of Rhett's secret rooms, I guess I'll need to reevaluate. There's no secret about the fact that I was angry with Georgia that night, but I didn't kill her. In fact, I never left the party, which is verifiable, so I suppose that gives me an alibi. Georgia stormed out and Rhett went after her. He was gone for a long time. I finally sent Jedd to look for him."

"And Dru?"

"He left shortly after Rhett did. When Dru didn't come back, I assumed he killed her and fled, but now? I suppose anyone could have had the opportunity to do it, but only a few of us had motive."

"Who do you feel had motive?" I asked.

"Beside myself? Rhett, I suppose. Georgia was flaunting Dru in his face the entire weekend, and he was gone for more than enough time. I've tried to be objective, to ask myself if I really believed Rhett would do such a thing. I have a hard time believing he would kill anyone, but he did seem to be hiding something after that weekend. I always assumed he helped Dru get away and, in fact, knew where he was. It was the idea that he was harboring the person who killed my sister that made me divorce him in the first place."

"What if Dru didn't die on the same night Georgia did? What if he didn't die until several years later?"

Hillary paused. "Is that what happened?"

"Off the record, yes. It looks like Dru died around the same time Rhett sold the property."

"That makes perfect sense, actually. A lot more sense than Rhett killing Georgia."

"If Dru did kill Georgia and took off to avoid arrest, as we assume, why do you think he came back?"

"To get his trunk."

"His trunk?" I asked.

"Dru had a locked trunk he kept on the estate. I don't know what was in it, but he was very protective of it. He had it hidden in one of the secret rooms, and only he knew the combination to unlock it. I imagine once he found out Rhett had sold the place, he realized his opportunity to retrieve his stuff was limited, so he came back for what he'd left behind."

"Do you think Rhett knew he was on the island?"

"Probably. He's also probably the one who informed him that he'd better get his property if he wanted it. I don't know for a fact that Rhett helped Dru escape that night and whether he stayed in contact with him after that, but I strongly suspect he did."

If nothing else, Hillary was confirming what we already suspected. "Who do you think killed Dru?" I asked.

"I have no idea. I wish I could be of more help, but he'd been gone a long time. It doesn't make sense that anyone other than his brother would know he'd come back."

I spoke to Hillary for a few more minutes, then hung up, after promising to call Alex that evening to fill him in on what was happening.

"Was the ex-wife helpful?" Garrett asked.

"Maybe. She didn't know who killed Dru, but she did say he most likely came back to the island for a trunk. If that's true and he never left the property alive, where's the trunk?"

"Good question. If the trunk had something valuable in it, the person who killed Dru could have taken it."

"If Dru was the only one who had the combination to the room where the trunk was hidden, and he opened the door, which allowed the trunk to be stolen, he must either have trusted the person who killed him or someone showed up when the door was already open, killed Dru, and took the trunk."

"If it was someone showing up afterward, not with him from the start, it seems to me it would have to be someone who lived on the island. Maybe someone who saw him and stopped to see what was going on."

"The neighbor," I realized.

"Claudia?"

"Do you know her?"

"Yeah, I know her. I wouldn't say we were friends, but we've chatted from time to time. She's not one to get involved, but she does help with the turtle rescue and has even come to a few meetings. She seems like a nice woman. Not the sort to kill a man and steal his treasure."

"I didn't pick up that vibe when I spoke to her either. Still, it might not hurt to follow up on the idea that even if she didn't do it, she might have seen something. If it wasn't her, maybe it was Wylie Slater."

"Why would Wylie kill Dru?"

"There's a theory floating around that Wylie had a thing for Georgia. She visited the estate fairly often, so they would have known each other. She was a young woman and he was a young man…"

"You think they had a thing going on?" Garrett asked.

"Maybe. And if they did, he might have felt the need to avenge her death. Everyone—including Wylie, I suspect—thinks Dru killed Georgia. If Wylie knew Dru was back, it's conceivable he might have confronted him and stabbed him to death during that confrontation."

"I don't know about that," Garrett said with a frown. "Your theory isn't totally far-fetched, but I don't see Wylie hurting anyone."

"That's what Savage said when I postulated the idea that Wylie had killed Georgia."

"You think he killed Georgia as well?"

"It's a theory, although not a strong one. Two people are dead, someone killed them, and the list of suspects is limited. Wylie knew both Dru and Georgia. He knew his way around the estate as well as anyone. He was the one who discovered Georgia's body in the toolshed at almost midnight. It's reasonable he would be on the suspect list at the very least."

"Maybe," Garrett agreed. "But I'll still be surprised if it turns out he did anything wrong."

******

After I left Garrett, I headed back into town to see if I could track down Savage. If I was going to spend time looking for a trunk in a hidden room, I wanted his blessing and possibly his help. As I'd learned, the house had had a lot of hidden rooms, but if any of them still had held a trunk, the demolition crew would have noticed. That meant the trunk was no longer on the property, or that it was hidden somewhere in the wing not yet demolished, or it was somewhere underground and thus not readily apparent during the demolition process.

Deputy Savage wasn't in his office, so I left him a voice mail letting him know what I'd learned and drove back to the estate to take another look around. I didn't have a lot of time before I needed to get home to get ready for my date with Jack, but my curiosity had been piqued and I wanted to take another look at the overall layout of the place. I wanted to speak to Claudia again too, but I didn't have time for a social call, so that would have to wait until the following day.

I took a quick walk around the perimeter of the grounds. It had been a magnificent house; too bad they'd torn it down. I was tempted to check out the remaining wing, but I was concerned it was no longer structurally sound. I wasn't sure where to begin to look beneath the rubble, but then I remembered the key. If Dru kept his treasures in a trunk, it made sense it would be locked. The key we'd found in the rubble seemed to indicate that he'd had it on him when his body was placed in the secret room. And if someone had killed Dru to steal whatever was in the trunk, they'd have taken the key. Maybe the trunk was still somewhere on the property after all.

The problem was that Hillary had indicated the trunk was in a secret room. If the room was aboveground, it would be exposed when the house came down. If the room had been underground, as I suspected, we'd need to find the opening among the rubble, which wasn't going to be easy, and not a task I would be able to accomplish by myself.

I took a last look around before leaving. I was beginning to get nervous about my date with Jack and was contemplating the idea of canceling it when I noticed something reflecting off a ray of the setting sun. I squinted against the glare as I carefully made my way to the spot where I'd noticed the flash of light. I bent down and lifted the top brick. Beneath it was a mirror, which, I realized, had been partially exposed even before I moved anything and, most likely, was what had reflected the light. Chances were the mirror wasn't any more significant than any other piece of debris, but I found it odd that we'd found a knife, a necklace, a key, and a mirror buried within the rubble. I wondered if they'd been left behind by the movers or if they'd been brought to the property afterward. The mirror probably had been in some room in the house and of no significance. It was also likely Dru had brought the key and the killer had brought the knife. Could the killer have brought the necklace as well? And if so, could identifying the necklace lead to the killer?

Chapter 9

I wasn't sure what to expect from my first-ever *real* date with Jack. He'd said to dress casually, so I assumed we weren't going anywhere fancy. He'd also said I should bring a sweatshirt, so that suggested we would be outdoors at least part of the time. I had no reason to be as nervous as I was. It wasn't as if I'd never been on a first date, and Jack wasn't a total stranger. We were friends. Maybe, I realized, being friends was the reason for the butterflies that were fluttering in my stomach.

Jack had said to wear jeans, so I slipped into a newer pair, topped it with a deep orange blouse that seemed to fit with the fall weather, then grabbed a dark brown sweater to top it all off. I let my long hair hang straight, then slipped my feet into a new pair of sandals. I decided to bring along a pair of tennis shoes as well as a pair of pumps in case I'd misread the situation.

Tossing everything, along with my wallet and house key, into a backpack, I headed downstairs to wait for Jack.

"Going out?" Brit, who was standing in front of the bookshelf browsing, asked.

"Dinner with Jack to discuss the case." I'm not sure why I felt I had to add the discuss-the-case part, but it seemed important to me that no one know this was a date.

"I was going to wait until the meeting tomorrow to fill you in, but I may have a lead on Honey Golden. She got married and her new name is Honey Tyson. She and her husband live in Atlanta. She was at the party as Jedd's date, and as far as I can tell looking at her past social media output, she didn't seem to be close to the Crawfords, but it couldn't hurt to chat with her. I sent her an instant message asking if she would be willing to talk. I'm waiting to hear from her."

"That's fantastic, Brit. You really know how to track someone down."

"Everyone leaves a trail on social media. You just need to backtrack to pick up the scent. Once you have that, you just follow the posts, tweets, and chats wherever they take you."

"Do you think it would be as easy to track down an item as it is to track down a person?"

"I guess it depends on the item."

"I found a necklace in the rubble out at the estate. It looks expensive. Most likely one of a kind."

"Can I see it?"

"Yeah. Come upstairs with me."

I jogged up the stairs with Brit on my heels. When we arrived at my attic bedroom, I retrieved the necklace from a drawer and handed it to Brit.

"It's beautiful. And I agree it's most likely custom made. I can't promise I can track down the source, but I'll try. Can I take a photo of it?"

"Sure, go ahead."

"Do you think maybe it belonged to Hillary Crawford?"

"Maybe. But it also seems possible it belonged to the killer. We found it near the spot where we found the murder weapon. Or at least we believe it to be the murder weapon."

Brit took photos of both the front and the back of the necklace from several different angles with her phone. "You think the person who killed Dru was a woman?"

"Perhaps. There's no way to know for certain at this point; it's a theory. The necklace may not lead anywhere, but I figured it was worth having a look."

"I agree. I'll let you know what I can find." Brit looked out the window. "Looks like Jack's here. I'm going to my cabin to do research and you have fun on your date."

I picked up my backpack and headed down the stairs and out the front door. Jack had just opened his car door when I arrived, so I motioned for him not to bother to get out.

"I would have picked you up at the door."

"No need." I slipped into the passenger side of the car. "Where are we going?"

"It's a surprise."

I'm not one to enjoy ambiguity, but now I just went with it, settling back into the soft leather of the car seat and preparing to enjoy the ride. I figured Jack was taking me to a casual restaurant and was surprised when we ended up at the marina.

"We're going on a dinner cruise?"

"No. Not a cruise."

"Are we renting a boat?"

Jack shook his head. "Not renting."

"You own a boat?"

"Yes. I don't get out on it as often as I'd like, but it seems to be a perfect evening for a short trip to watch the sun set."

Jack was right; it was a perfect night to be on the water. It was calm and clear, with just the smallest hint of crispness in the air. Jack took my hand and led me down the dock to the part of the marina where the larger boats were kept. When he stopped in front of a boat that could only be referred to as a yacht, I let my mouth hang open.

"This is your boat?"

"This is *Francesca*."

I stood in awe as Jack hopped onto the deck of the large vessel.

"I assume the yacht is named after a woman?"

"She is."

"Okay, who's Francesca?" I asked.

Jack put out his hand to help me aboard. "That's actually a funny story I think better suited for another time. Why don't you head belowdeck and look around while I tell the captain to shove off? I want to be sure to make it out onto the open sea before sunset. It should be a beautiful one today."

"There's a captain?"

"For tonight."

I had to admit I was impressed. Not only was there a dining area as well as a tanning and lounging area on the deck but there were three cabins, a bathroom, and a good-sized kitchen and dining area belowdeck. One could travel around the world in a boat this size if they wanted to. I wondered if Jack had taken it on an extensive sea journey.

"All set," Jack said after joining me a few minutes later. "I thought we could have some wine and watch the sun set before we eat."

"Sounds perfect. I can't believe you own a yacht and you've never once mentioned it."

He shrugged. "I guess it never came up in conversation. Until recently, I had it docked near my house on the Cape, but I never made it there last summer, so I decided to move it."

"You own a house on the Cape?"

"I do. I'd love for you to see it sometime. Maybe we could go for a long weekend. In fact, now would be the perfect time to visit. The tourists have gone and it's nice and quiet."

Suddenly, I felt like I was on a date with Jackson Jones, superrich megastar, rather than Jack from the newspaper. I found I wasn't sure I liked that feeling at all.

"Let's head up to the deck," I suggested without committing one way or the other to his invitation to the Cape. "We wouldn't want to miss the sunset."

As it turned out, the sunset was as spectacular as we thought it would be. The gentle rocking of the sea, combined with Jack's expensive wine and the ultracushy double lounge we were seated on eventually managed to chase away my trepidations so that I was having a good time. By the time the small Christmas-style lights came on around the perimeter of the deck, I was totally engrossed in the perfection of the moment.

“Dinner is ready, sir,” a man dressed in a white captain’s uniform announced.

“Thank you, Paul. We’ll be right there.”

“The captain cooks?” I asked.

“More like serves. We’re eating picnic style tonight. I hope that’s okay.”

“It sounds perfect.”

We got up from the lounge and headed to the table that was set up with two place settings as well as candles and flowers. Jack helped me into my chair before removing the covering from a platter, revealing several different cheeses, sliced fruit, and crackers. Another platter featured smoked salmon, large shrimp, and ahi layered on fresh greens. A loaf of crispy fresh bread and several spreads rounded up the offerings.

“This looks delicious.”

“Wine?” Jack asked, holding up a chilled bottle of white.

“Please.” After the wine we’d had on the deck, I knew I should probably pass on more with dinner, but somehow, I found I didn’t care about avoiding a headache in the morning. “So, tell me something about you I don’t know.”

“Like what?” Jack asked.

I shrugged. “I don’t know. One thing you’re proud of and one you’re embarrassed by.”

“Okay.” Jack bit into one of the plump shrimp. “Let’s see. I’m proud of the fact that I was the chess champion for my state when I was a junior in high school and I’m embarrassed that my spelling is so bad I go out of my way to avoid handwriting letters of any kind. As far as I’m concerned, Spell Check is the greatest thing ever invented.”

"Your spelling is really that bad?"

"It is, but hey, chess champion. That's pretty awesome, right?"

I laughed. "It *is* pretty awesome. I never learned to play. You'll have to teach me sometime."

Jack's grin grew lopsided. "I'll teach you anything you're willing to learn, pretty lady. More wine?"

I held out my glass and let him top it off.

"Now it's your turn," Jack said. "One thing you're proud of and one you're embarrassed by."

I picked up a piece of cheese while I considered the questions. I wasn't sure where Jack had bought his supplies, but so far this was the most delicious picnic I'd ever eaten. "I guess I'm proudest of the national award I won for a short story I wrote when I was ten."

Jack raised an eyebrow. "Impressive. What was it about?"

"A lonely little girl who creates a fantasy world to compensate for the lack of human interaction in her life only to find out she'd somehow become trapped there and can't get back to her real life."

"What happened?"

"Most of the story is about the girl trying to get home. During her journey, she realizes that despite the imperfection of her real life and the people who've let her down, she values it quite a lot. Each revelation she receives along the way leads her just a bit closer to her goal."

"Does she ever make it home?"

"Yes, although by the time she finally gets there, she's forever changed. She no longer looks externally for security and companionship. She realizes all she really needs to survive in the often-harsh world is herself."

Jack put his hand over mine and gave it a squeeze. "It sounds like a great story. I'd like to read it someday."

I blushed, suddenly feeling I had revealed more than I intended. "Maybe someday."

"And how about something you find embarrassing?" Jack asked.

Spilling my guts to a man who I suddenly want to kiss more than I can remember wanting anything else.

"I sometimes drool in my sleep," I blurted out.

Jack laughed. "I bet you're adorable when you sleep. Drool and all."

"So I've been told." I winked in an effort to quell my growing desire to jump across the table and follow through on my fantasies about Jack's lips. "As fun as this has been, I think we should head back."

"It's early," Jack countered.

"I know, but I'm meeting Deputy Savage pretty early."

"You're meeting Savage?"

"We found out about a trunk Dru may have been returning to the estate to retrieve when he was killed. We're meeting in the morning to look for it. You are, of course, invited to join us if you'd like."

Jack looked momentarily disappointed in the change of subject but quickly recovered. "I think I can arrange things so I can meet up with you. How'd you find out about the trunk?"

"Hillary Crawford." I filled Jack in on my conversation with her. The more I focused on the case, the less vulnerable I felt. Jack seemed like a good guy, but there was no way I wanted to make room for a relationship at this point in my life.

"It seems if there'd been something as large as a trunk left on the property, it would have been found by now," Jack said.

"Maybe," I answered. "But there's still that one wing that hasn't been demolished, and it occurred to me that at least some of the secret passages could be underground."

"Yes, but the entrances to the belowground passages would most likely have been aboveground."

"True, but it can't hurt to look around. I have no idea if finding the trunk will help to lead to Dru's killer, but it would be nice to figure this out and wrap up the story."

"I agree that looking for the trunk might be worth our time, but I also feel we should try to complete the interviews before tomorrow night's Mystery Mastermind meeting."

"Mystery Mastermind?" I asked.

"That's what I've been calling the group to myself. I hope you don't mind."

"I don't mind. In fact, I like it; let's use the name. Okay, so what's the plan for completing the interviews?"

"Of the twelve people on the estate on the night of Georgia's murder, Georgia and Dru are dead. We've spoken to Hillary, Tiffany, Claudia, and Olivia, which leaves Rhett, Jedd, Honey, Reggie, Trent, and Wylie."

"Wylie is out to sea, as far as I know, and Victoria is working on getting a meeting with Rhett and/or Jedd," I reminded Jack. "Brit has a message out to Honey, which leaves Tiffany's date, Reggie Southern, and Claudia's date, Trent Truitt. Trent lives on Folly Island and Reggie lives in Charleston."

"I'll see if I can get in touch with them. If they agree to interviews, we can see them after we help Savage look for the trunk in the morning. If you're free, that is."

"I'm free. I'll call Vikki when I get home to see if she has any news regarding Rhett and Jedd. Maybe by the time the Mastermind group meets tomorrow we'll have all we need to come up with a viable theory that will just need to be authenticated."

"Sounds like a plan." Jack threw his head back and looked up at the zillions of stars in the sky. "As perfect as this is, I guess we should head back, as you suggested. I'll alert the captain."

"Jack…"

"Yes?"

"I really did have a good time. In fact, as far as first dates go, I think this is my very favorite one."

Jack smiled. "Did you enjoy it enough to try a second date?"

I paused and then replied, "Let's solve this case and then we can talk about it. If nothing else, a celebratory dinner might be in order."

Jack walked around the table and pulled me to my feet. He leaned forward just a bit and gently placed his lips on mine. It was a gentle kiss that ended way too soon, but it seemed to hold a promise of something more to come.

Chapter 10

Thursday, October 26

By the time I'd made my way down the stairs the following morning, Clara had built a fire and brewed a pot of tea. Normally, I'm an early riser, but between the wine I'd drunk the night before and the chilly drizzle falling from the sky outside my bedroom window, it felt like a good day to sleep in. Of course, I wouldn't be able to linger by the fire too long; Jack would be by to pick me up in less than an hour for the meeting with Deputy Savage at the Crawford place. I realized finding the trunk Hillary had mentioned was a long shot, but it wasn't as if we had much else to go on.

"Would you like some tea, dear?" Clara asked as I wandered over to stand by the fire.

"Thank you, I would. Seems like a hot tea sort of day."

"It's my own blend, guaranteed to ward off any ill effects from a bit of overindulgence."

I had no idea how Clara knew I'd overindulged, but I was happy for the tea and simply smiled as I looked out the window at the dark sky. Based on the look of things, we were in for a wet and windy day. I just hoped it let up a bit before we were supposed to meet Savage. I had a rain slicker that would keep my clothes dry, but I wasn't looking forward to digging through rubble as rain dripped down my face.

"I was able to pick up a bit more information on the third victim I've been sensing," Clara said as she handed me a cup.

"That's great," I said as I accepted it. "What do you know?"

"The victim was a woman. I'm sensing someone young at the time of her death. Maybe in her twenties. I'm also sensing she died before the others, yet she's connected to the estate, or perhaps the individuals who owned the estate, or at least stayed there on a regular basis."

"You said the woman died before the others. Do you know how much before?" I asked.

Clara shook her head. "I'm not sure. At least not yet."

I took a sip of tea and let it warm me on the inside. "The woman is connected to either the people who owned the estate or the estate itself. Could she have lived there before the Crawfords owned it? Or perhaps she was related to the previous owner."

Clara paused and then said, "No, I don't think so. While I feel she died before the others, I sense she was in some way connected to young Ms. Darcy. I'm not sure whether they knew each other or if they died in proximity to each other."

"Or if they were killed by the same person?"

"Perhaps. It's all still a bit confusing at this point, but I sense betrayal. And pain. Not just physical pain but emotional pain."

"I suppose if this woman was murdered she would feel a sense of betrayal. Do you think she died in the house?"

"I think she might have, but I can't be certain. If I were you, I'd do a search to see if anyone died in the house prior to Ms. Darcy but after Mr. Crawford bought the place. If not, I'd look for people associated with the Crawfords who died during the time between when Mr. Crawford bought the house and his sister-in-law's death there. Perhaps a relative or even a love interest."

"I'll ask Deputy Savage about it, and if he doesn't have anything, Jack and I will search through old newspaper articles. Does anything stand out about the woman? Maybe a name or hair color?"

"I'm not getting a name, but I sense she had long dark hair and blue eyes."

"Okay. That gives us a place to start. I'm going to be gone for a good part of the day, but I'll be back before our meeting tonight. In the meantime, if you think of something else, call or text me."

"There's one thing," Clara added as I finished my tea. "I sense that someone you'll speak with today will lie to you. The lie will be buried with half-truths, but if you aren't careful, it will lead you down a dangerous path."

"A dangerous path? What do you mean by that? Will I be in danger or will I put someone else in danger?'

"I'm not sure. I'll consult my cards. Perhaps I can get a clearer vision of the danger I can only sense at this point." Clara looked me in the eye. "I've grown quite fond of you since we've shared this earthly space. In many ways, you're the daughter I never had. Do be careful as you seek your answers."

"I will. I promise." I thanked Clara for the tea and hurried upstairs to get ready for the day ahead.

******

Thankfully, the rain had stopped at least temporarily by the time Jack and I arrived on the estate. Deputy Savage was already there, so I pulled on my rain slicker and we headed toward the rubble. Today we were looking specifically for a trunk or evidence of one, which would still be difficult to find given the situation, but at least this was more focused than digging through rubble with no specific goal in mind.

"Any luck?" I asked as I joined Savage near the far corner of the rubble pile.

"Maybe. I found an opening just below the spot where I'm working. It looks like the entrance to an underground passage, although I can't know for certain if it's intact until I clear away some of this debris."

"We'll help you," I offered, and I dug in. Today I'd thought to bring gloves to protect my hands from the sharp objects hidden in the pile.

"And I called to speak to Hillary Crawford," Savage said. "She indicated that Dru's suite was in the north wing of the house, which happens to be the one that used to be where we're standing. Apparently, he had an underground room that was protected by a steel door locked with a code only he knew. If we can find the door, I have explosives in the car that will help us gain access without the code."

"Explosives?" I screeched. Suddenly I had a vision of Hiroshima.

"They'll provide a small, focused explosion that will blow out the door and other areas not easily accessible. Don't worry; I've been trained in the proper handling. We'll be perfectly safe."

I certainly hoped so. Savage didn't seem like the reckless sort, so I guessed I'd have to take his word for the fact that he knew what he was doing.

"This is also where we found the knife. Did you manage to pull DNA or prints from it?" I asked.

"The blood is definitely Dru Breland's, but the handle had been wiped clean. The forensic guys are still working on it, but I doubt they'll find anything that would point to the identity of his killer."

"What about the room where his body was found?" I asked.

Savage pointed to where debris already had been cleared away. "The body was found over there and the area was thoroughly searched at the time. We didn't find anything other than the body. A lack of blood indicates the body was moved from the murder scene and stashed in the room. I still haven't figured out whether the killer didn't realize the house was going to be torn down or did know and didn't care." Savage set a large brick aside, then leaned further into the hole we'd uncovered.

"Do you see anything?" I asked.

"There are stairs leading into the ground. It looks like the floor of the passage is maybe six feet below ground level. It's reinforced with a steel frame, so I'm guessing it will be safe to walk on." Savage turned and looked at Jack and me. "I'll go and you wait here, just in case something happens and I need someone to dig me out."

"Do you have a flashlight?" Jack asked.

Savage held one up, then disappeared into the hole. I figured the passage couldn't be all that long, so we'd know if there was anything there within a few minutes. It seemed I was correct; less than a minute later, Savage poked his head back out of the hole.

"I found the locked door. I'll get the explosives. It'll be tricky to get the door open without caving the whole thing in, but it seems like our best bet."

Jack and I waited while Savage went to his car for the explosives. It had begun to drizzle again, and I pulled my hood up over my hair. I had a feeling I was going to look like a drowned rat by the end of the day.

"The surf is really pounding today," Jack said loudly over the sound of the crashing waves.

"I suppose that's a good thing. The waves should help drown out the explosion. We probably don't want to attract the interest of the neighbors."

"The closest neighbor is Claudia, and she's pretty far away," Jack pointed out.

"True. I guess in my mind, Savage plans some huge blast, while it will probably be just a little pop."

Jack nodded behind me. "We'll soon find out. Here he comes."

Savage counseled Jack and me to stand well away before he went back down into the hole, so we took a position behind a pile of rubble. A few minutes later, Savage came running back out and joined us. There was a small poof of dust and only a tiny sound that would totally have been missed if I hadn't been listening for it.

Once the dust had cleared, Savage headed back down the hole. When he emerged again, he said, "I was able to open the door, which led to a narrow passage that opens into a larger room. The entire structure is steel-reinforced. I found the trunk in the larger room, but I can't open it. I'll need something to break the lock."

"Wait; I have a key." I reached into my pocket and pulled out the small key Blackbeard had led me to. "I found it when I was here the first time. I don't know for certain it goes to this trunk, but it seems it's the right size to open one."

Savage held out his hand and I put it in his palm. He disappeared back down into the hole and a couple of minutes later I heard a shout. "What the hell!"

I glanced at Jack, then back at the hole. "I'm going down. I'll come right back to tell you what's going on."

Jack nodded and I climbed down. I took out my flashlight and slowly made my way through the now-open door and down the long, narrow tunnel, wondering exactly who'd built the tunnel and what it had been for. As Savage had indicated, it opened into a larger room, where I found him standing over the open trunk. "What is it?" I asked him.

Savage stepped aside. I gasped when I realized the trunk held a skeleton. A human skeleton.

"The third victim," I said.

"Third victim?" Savage asked.

"Clara told me this morning there was a third death associated with the house or the people who lived there. A young woman with long, dark hair and blue eyes."

Savage looked back at the body. "I can't tell you if this woman had dark hair and blue eyes, but I can verify the skeleton was a female. I need to get the trunk out of here and the remains to the crime lab. I have no idea who this woman was, but if this was Dru's trunk, I'm thinking Georgia wasn't the first young woman he murdered."

"You think he was some sort of serial killer?"

Savage shrugged. "Maybe. Or maybe he just had a temper and was prone to fits of anger and aggression. Either way, with a second body found in the house, there's no way the sheriff's going to be able to block a thorough investigation of the entire property."

"Did you ever figure out his reason for not doing a more thorough search when Dru's body was found?"

Savage narrowed his gaze. "No, and that bothers me more than I care to admit. If I didn't know him better, I'd say he was on the take, but that just doesn't fit. Let's get this body out of here. The sooner we find out who this is, the sooner we're likely to figure everything out."

We returned to the surface and Savage called in the help he needed, while Jack and I decided to go ahead with our plans for the day. Not only had the deputy phoned for a crime scene unit but cadaver dogs were on the way, in the event there were additional bodies to find. It looked as if the CSI people were going to remove every piece of debris slowly and individually, which seemed like a long, tedious task, and I was just as happy to leave it to them.

"I have to say I didn't expect to find a body when we set out to look for the trunk today," Jack said as we drove to Folly Island to meet Trent Truitt, the first of the two interviews we had set up for the day.

"Yeah, me neither. I wonder who she was."

"People don't usually just disappear without anyone noticing. Chances are there's a missing persons report that will match the remains."

I scrunched up my nose. "Doesn't it seem odd to you that Dru would keep a body in a trunk? I mean, even if he killed that poor girl, why wouldn't he bury her or dump her in the ocean? It makes no sense for him to have kept her."

"Unless he was obsessed with her," Jack suggested.

"I guess. If he kept her on the island, he must have killed her here. He wouldn't have killed her in Los Angeles and then transported her body all the way to the East Coast. When I asked around, it did seem like he visited Gull Island often, even when his brother didn't. I can't remember if anyone ever said when Rhett bought the estate."

"Eleven years ago," Jack supplied. "I looked it up right after that first day we discussed the case."

"Clara indicated the third victim she sensed was the first death, which means the girl in the trunk was killed before Georgia. If the remains aren't easily identifiable, I bet the Crawfords can help put together a timeline. They must have an idea when the trunk arrived on the property."

Jack made a right and turned onto the main highway before saying, "It occurred to me that Rhett or Hillary or both might have been in on the cover-up. I mean, it does seem odd that Dru would have this trunk hidden on their property without them demanding to know what was in it."

"Hillary thinks Rhett helped Dru get away after he killed Georgia," I informed Jack. "He may have helped him hide the first body as well."

"I guess that could make sense. They're brothers, and siblings sometimes do things for each other they wouldn't otherwise do. Do you have the directions for the restaurant where Trent wanted to meet?"

"Just stay on this road for another five miles and then take the first left after the gas station. I'll warn you when you get closer."

Our conversation for the next few minutes involved me giving directions and him asking about the questions I felt we should ask during our interview. After everything we'd already learned, I was pretty sure we had a good grip on what had happened the night Georgia died, but we'd already made the appointment, so I figured we may as well follow up.

Trent was sitting in a large booth eating a club sandwich when we arrived. He was a nice-looking man who looked to be in his early forties. I remembered he'd worked as a contractor, and he seemed to be doing well for himself. We introduced ourselves and sat down across from him. Jack asked a few general questions and then I filled him in on the information we'd uncovered so far.

"Dru didn't kill Georgia," Trent countered the moment I shared our theory that Dru had killed her and Rhett had helped him escape.

"How can you be so sure of that?" I asked.

"I was with him."

I frowned. "You were with him the entire time? Not a single person has mentioned you even left the room."

"I was a no one at that party. A fly on the wall. I was a guest of a guest who hadn't been part of the mix until that evening. With all the drama and star power in the room, a person who was easily overlooked. Even my date barely noticed I was there."

"Had you been dating Claudia long?"

"No. Claudia needed a date for the party and a mutual friend set us up. I hadn't even met her until a few days before the party and we never went out again after it."

I glanced at Jack, who shrugged and then took out his little notebook. "Okay," I began, "tell me what you remember about that night."

"Like I said, I was a guest of a guest, so I didn't have all the background, nor did I particularly care about the drama surrounding whom was sleeping with whom. I spent most of the night that young woman died getting hammered. It was a hot evening, and by the time dinner was over, I had a pounding headache, so I went outside to get some fresh air. I was sitting in the garden nursing a whiskey when Georgia came storming out of the house. A few minutes later, Rhett Crawford came running out after her."

"And then?" I asked.

Trent shrugged. "I don't know. I didn't see where they went. To be honest, I didn't care. About twenty minutes after Rhett took off after Georgia, Dru came outside. He was not only madder than a dog who'd gotten his tail stuck in the screen door but he was almost as drunk as I was. He saw me nursing my bottle and sat down next to me. We finished it off and then headed into town. The party had become a lot more drama-infused than either of us wanted to deal with, so we decided to go to a bar."

"Do you remember what time you arrived at the bar?" I asked.

"I guess around eleven."

"And what time did you leave?"

The man scratched his head. "I don't know. It was late. The bar was closing. Dru had passed out in the booth where we were sitting, so I carried him out, dumped him in his car, and went home."

I paused to let that sink in. "So if Dru didn't kill Georgia, why did he take off? The sheriff's department assumed he was guilty of the murder because he took off the way he did."

"I don't know. I'd never met him before that night and I never saw him again. Hell, I was so stinking drunk I barely remember what we talked about."

"Are you sure about the time you dumped him in his car? Could it have been earlier?"

"Yeah, I'm sure. Like I said, the bar was closing. If it hadn't been, I probably would have just left him in the booth and let him sleep it off there."

"Which bar did you go to?" Jack asked.

Trent frowned. "I think it was called the Pink Pelican, or maybe it was the Pink Parrot. I'm not sure. Dru picked the bar, which turned out to be one I'd never been in before. I do know it's closed down now."

"It was on Gull Island?"

"Yeah. On the west side of town. They tore down the building and built that new restaurant with all the big windows in its place."

I knew exactly which restaurant Trent was referring to. If Savage wanted to follow up with the owner or bartender, he could track him down, assuming he was still on the island.

"If you left the party before Georgia's body was found, were you ever interviewed by anyone from the sheriff's department?"

"Yeah. A guy came by my house the next day."

"Did you tell him what you just told us?"

"I was so hung over when he came by, I couldn't tell you much about the interview."

"Was the man who interviewed you Deputy Savage?"

"No. It was some other guy. I don't remember his name. I think he was from the county office."

We spoke to Trent a while longer, but he didn't have any additional information of relevance. He stuck to his position of general ignorance of the interactions that took place that evening, claiming inebriation as his excuse for his lack of clarity. I wasn't certain I believed his story. I couldn't see why he'd lie, but his story deviated completely from every other one I'd been told.

"Everyone has said Dru left the party and never came back," Jack said. "We assumed he didn't because he was killing Georgia Darcy and then fleeing the island, but what if he really was getting smashed with Trent?"

"If that's true, why didn't he come back to the estate when he sobered up? And where was he for the four years between Georgia's death and his?"

Jake shook his head. "I'm afraid I don't have an answer for that one."

I took a deep breath, trying to clear my head. Every time I thought we were getting somewhere, we were back at square one.

"In my opinion, Trent's story feels like a fabrication," I added. "He doesn't have any proof that any of it actually happened, and don't you think it's just a little too convenient that the bar he says he was in with Dru has closed down?"

"I agree Trent's statement doesn't ring true."

"Clara warned me that someone was going to lie to me today. She said I needed to be careful because the lie could lead to danger. I'm not sure how Trent's lie could be dangerous, but I guess we can ask Claudia whether Trent was there when Georgia's body was found. It doesn't sound like Trent even told her he was leaving."

"I'll call her to see if we can stop by later," Jack offered. "At the least, maybe she'll answer a few questions over the phone."

"Okay, but for now, let's continue on to Charleston to see what Reggie Southern has to say. He might have a different take on things. Then I want to call Savage after we talk to him. Maybe he can check the interview the deputy from the county office conducted with Trent the day after the murder. And he may have news on the skeleton."

Chapter 11

When Jack had called Reggie Southern to ask if he'd be willing to speak to us, he'd said he was working from his home office that week, but it was fine if we came by. The rain was coming down harder by the time we pulled up in front of the nice house in an upscale neighborhood, close enough to the door that we only needed to make a short sprint to it. The porch was covered, so we didn't get soaked while we waited for Reggie to answer our knock.

"You must be Jack and Jill," a tall man with dark hair and thick, rimmed glasses said when he answered the door.

"Jack Jones." Jack stuck out his hand. "We appreciate your taking time out of your busy day to speak to us."

"I'm happy to help if I can." He took a step back and indicated that we should come inside. "I have a fire going in the living room if you'll follow me this way."

He led us there, then gestured to the sofa and offered us coffee, which I declined but Jack accepted.

The men chatted about the fishing trophy on the mantel for a few minutes before Jack brought things around to the reason we were there.

"Sure, I remember that night," Reggie said. "Tiffany was invited to the party and asked me if I'd go with her. I almost said no; the sort of parties the Crawfords had a reputation for throwing weren't really my thing, but Tiff didn't have anyone else to go with and she didn't want to go alone. Eventually, I gave in and went."

"Did you know anyone else at the party?" I asked.

"I didn't know any of the other guests, but I did know the groundskeeper, a guy named Wylie Slater. We hung out at the same bar and had played on the same softball team."

"And where was Wylie on the night of the party?" Jack asked.

"He wasn't invited to the party, but he was working that night. I noticed him coming through a few times to clear dishes and restock the bar. I imagine he was hanging out in the little cabin he lived in when he wasn't needed. I don't know where he was for certain."

"Were you there when Wylie came in and announced he'd found Georgia's body in the toolshed?" I asked.

"Yes."

"Do you remember who else was in the room at the time?"

Reggie tapped his chin with his forefinger. "Mr. and Mrs. Crawford were there. She was obviously extremely distraught, as was her husband. Tiffany and I were chatting with a woman named Claudia Norris at the time. I think Mr. Crawford's friend Jedd was there as well. Beyond that, I'm not certain. People were drifting between the house and the patio all evening."

"What about Trent Truitt?" I asked.

"The guy who was there with Claudia Norris?"

I nodded.

"He and I both felt pretty out of place, so we'd chatted earlier in the evening, but I don't think he was in the room when Wylie came in. He may have stepped out. I do remember he was pretty hammered."

"And Dru Breland?" I asked.

"He left shortly after Georgia did and never came back. I think everyone assumed he was the one who killed her. He was not only totally sloshed but he was a total jerk too. I had to struggle to control the urge to punch him more than once."

"He was a jerk how?" Jack asked.

"He was not only vulgar but loud. He treated every female there like dirt, and I could see the Crawfords were pretty disgusted with the way he was acting. When he finally left the room, everyone breathed a sigh of relief. That is, until we found out about the girl and realized he must have been off killing her when he left the party."

"One of the other guests told us Dru was with him in town at the time, so he couldn't have killed Georgia Darcy," I stated.

Reggie frowned. "In town? Why would he go into town?"

"It seems he was angry after his fight with Georgia and left."

"If he did, he didn't take the rental car he came in. The jerk was parked behind me and when he didn't come back I had to have it towed so I could get out of the driveway at the end of the evening."

I glanced at Jack, who narrowed his eyes. If Dru hadn't taken his car into town, Trent's statement that he'd left Dru in it when the bar closed couldn't be true—unless, of course, Dru had been driving a car other than his rental. I supposed we could ask Trent if he remembered what make and model Dru was driving that night, although his spotty recollections had been less than useful so far.

"If we take Dru out of the picture, who do you think was the most likely person to have killed Georgia Darcy?" Jack asked.

Reggie didn't answer right away. The serious look on his face made me think he was going over the party guests in his mind.

"I'm not sure. I know I didn't do it, and I was with Tiffany the entire evening, so I know she didn't do it either. Claudia Norris seemed to be around all the time as well, although I wasn't exactly tracking her every move. I remember Mrs. Crawford being around most of the evening, and I can't imagine her killing her own sister. She seemed genuinely shocked and remorseful when Wylie told us he'd found her body."

"She's an actress," I reminded him.

"True. But if she was faking it, she's a better actress than I ever gave her credit for. Rhett Crawford did leave us right after Georgia Darcy did, and he was gone for a long time. I suppose he could have done it, but I don't know why he would have with a house full of guests. Seems like he would have found a better hiding place to stash the body."

"I've wondered how it was that Wylie found Georgia's body. I mean, why would he even go in the toolshed at that time of the night?"

"Yes, I guess that was a little odd. You'll have to ask him."

Jack looked through his notes, reading a page, then flipping it over to the next. Finally, after glancing at four or five pages, he looked up. "The one person no one has really talked about is Honey Golden, Jedd Boswell's date."

"I don't remember seeing her much. I know everyone was there for dinner, but I'm pretty sure she left even before Georgia Darcy stormed off. She may not have been feeling well. I'm pretty sure she never came back to the party that night."

"And Jedd?" I asked.

"He was there. He was in and out, but he was around. I remember him holding Hillary while the cops interviewed Rhett. She was pretty hysterical, but for some reason she refused to go to her room. Maybe she didn't want to miss anything."

We spoke to Reggie for a while longer before saying our good-byes. I wasn't sure we were narrowing in on a suspect for Georgia Darcy's murder, but at this point my money was still on Dru despite what Trent had said.

"What do you think?" I asked Jack as we drove back to Gull Island.

"I think it might be too early to say for certain who killed Georgia, although we both suspect the killer will end up being Dru. Still, just in case we're wrong, maybe we should focus a bit. Rhett, Hillary, Dru, Jedd, Honey, Claudia, Tiffany, Reggie, Trent, Olivia, and Wylie were all on the grounds the night

Georgia was hit over the head and stuffed in the shed. Based on the interviews we've conducted thus far, I'd say we have no reason to suspect Olivia, Tiffany, or Reggie."

"So far, I agree."

"Trent didn't seem to know anyone there, including Georgia, so on the surface he would seem not to have a motive, but unless Dru really did leave with him, he's lying about what went down that night. I say he stays on the suspect list for now."

"Agreed. And I think Wylie should be on the list as well," I added. "It still seems odd to me that he'd just stumble on the body."

Jack nodded. "So we have Dru, Wylie, and Trent as suspects. I think Rhett needs to be on the list because we've not only been told by several people he was having an affair with Georgia but he's also the one who went after her when she took off."

"What about Hillary?" I asked.

Jack glanced at me. "You spoke to her. What's your impression?"

"I didn't pick up the vibe that she was lying, if that's what you're asking. I suppose she may have been angry enough to hit her sister when she found out she'd been sleeping with her husband, but that wouldn't make her a strong suspect. I guess if we have a maybe list, I'd put her there."

"Okay. That seems reasonable for now. Dru, Wylie, Trent, and Rhett are on the yes list; Olivia, Tiffany, and Reggie are on the no list; Hillary is on the maybe list. What about Jedd and Honey?"

"It isn't possible for me to have a feel for Honey right now," I said. "If Reggie is correct, she disappeared that night, but I have no idea if she had a motive. I guess you could put her on the maybe list with Jedd too, who may have had a thing for Georgia. Which just leaves Claudia, and I didn't pick up any red flags when we spoke."

Jack turned onto the road leading from the main highway to the islands. "We have the Mystery Mastermind meeting tonight. Let's see if anyone has found out anything else. Once all the cards are on the table, we can reevaluate the lists."

"Sounds like a good plan. I still want to call Savage, and I also want to touch base with Victoria, who was supposed to speak to Rhett and Jedd. In fact, I'll call everyone as soon as we get back to the island."

"I want to stop by the newspaper, but I can drop you off at the resort," Jack offered.

"That would probably work out best. I'll call you if I find out anything interesting."

******

Savage was busy when I called him, but he did say they hadn't identified the body we'd found that morning yet. There hadn't been any missing persons reports filed locally during the time the medical examiner estimated she had most likely been killed and there hadn't been any luck running a search based on dental records. I told him I had news to share, so he agreed to call me back when he could free up a few minutes.

Vikki likewise indicated she'd need to call me back because she was just going into a meeting with her agent, so I grabbed Blackbeard and took a short walk because the rain had cleared temporarily.

Of the twenty cabins I planned to renovate and rent to writers, three had been completed and George, Brit, and Alex had moved into them. An additional three were finished but waiting for inspection, and three others were in the process of being redone. Vikki wanted one of the cabins awaiting inspection, and there were two writers who'd filled out applications and could move in as early as the first of the year. Before I promised the cabins to them, though, I should check with Clara. She seemed happy in the main house, but we hadn't discussed things for some time, so an inquiry would probably be a good idea.

Blackbeard seemed happy to sit on my shoulder as we walked along the beach. I'd tied his tether to his leg so he wouldn't fly off on another of his adventures. He hadn't said much of anything since I'd taken him from his cage, so it startled me when he finally did speak.

"Hidden treasure, hidden treasure."

"I see you have a bit of the treasure-hunting fever that seems to enchant almost everyone on the island. I guess you know Garrett has a map. Someday, if I have the time, we can go look for hidden treasure. Would you like that?"

"Shiver me timbers, shiver me timbers."

I laughed. "I'll take that as a yes. Maybe Jack will want to come with us. The map leads to a treasure on another island, so we'll make a weekend out of it."

"Not a date, not a date."

"Exactly. I have to say, you're one smart bird."

When I'd first found out about the treasure map our father had hidden in the main house at the resort, I was intrigued but not overly interested in following up on it. It seemed like searching for hidden treasure was something you did in your mind, not in actuality. Since then, however, I'd chatted with Garrett about it during our weekly visits and he'd shared the history of the map. After hearing what others had gone through in the hope of finding the treasure, I'd become intrigued. But treasure hunting took time, which I hadn't had yet.

I was almost back to the house when my phone rang. I looked at the caller ID.

"Hey, Vikki. Thanks for calling me back. How did your meeting go?"

"Good. It looks like we have a deal for three of the books. My agent is working out the details, but at this point it seems to be a go."

"Are you still coming home this weekend?"

"Yeah. I've done what I can for the movies for now. I miss you guys."

I smiled. "We miss you too. I'm having a dinner party on the thirty-first. Just the gang plus a couple of folks from town. I'm glad you'll be back for it. It seems like forever since we had the whole group together."

"It has been a while. How are the cabins coming along?"

"The inspection for the next three is scheduled for next month. After the last easy one, I'm not expecting any problems. You should be able to move in once we get clearance."

"Great. I'm excited to have my own space. So about this mystery you're working on… I was able to meet with Jedd, but I haven't been able to get through to Rhett. He has an army of people between himself and the public, so unless you have an in of some sort, I'm not sure I'll be able to speak to him."

"Jedd couldn't get you hooked up?"

"Apparently, Jedd and Rhett had a falling-out and haven't spoken since shortly after the party. It seems Jedd's convinced Rhett was involved in the murder in some way, but he can't prove it."

"He thinks Rhett killed Georgia?" I clarified.

"He thinks he either killed her or knows who did and is protecting them. According to Jedd, Rhett was pretty mad when Georgia showed up at the party with Dru. It's his opinion Georgia knew Rhett would be upset when he found out his lover and his brother were sleeping together, so she brought him to the party intentionally to get back at him for not leaving Hillary and hooking up with her in a more public manner."

"Dru and Rhett are both on our list of suspects," I confirmed. "Did Jedd have an opinion about who might have killed Dru?"

"He wasn't sure. He said Dru was an odd sort who drank a lot and had a tendency toward violence. When Jedd found out he was dead, he wasn't surprised to find out someone had offed him, although he didn't think it was Rhett. He said Rhett felt responsible for Dru. He helped him out on many occasions, which is probably the only reason Dru didn't ended up in prison a long time ago."

"There's a theory floating around that Dru killed Georgia and Rhett helped him get off the island and basically disappear."

"Jedd had a similar theory, although he didn't know how Dru ended up in the secret room. At first, he thought Dru was killed on the night Georgia died, but Hillary called him to let him know he'd died four years later."

I entered the house and set Blackbeard on his perch. "So Hillary and Jedd have stayed in touch?"

"Yes. Jedd told me that Hillary didn't really like him much when she was married to Rhett because she felt he was a bad influence. But after Georgia died, Jedd was really there for her. More so than her own husband, who was dealing with the loss of his mistress. When she decided to divorce Rhett, Jedd helped her find a good attorney and then move across the country. It seems to me they're pretty close now."

I found that bit of information both interesting and relevant. I'd need to think about the ramifications of a Jedd/Hillary alliance once I had a few minutes to noodle on the situation.

"Did you happen to ask Jedd about Honey Golden?" I asked.

"I did. He said he met her on a movie set. She was a model who had a bit part in a beach scene and they got to talking. He invited her to the party on a whim because the woman he'd been dating had recently broken things off with him. According to Jedd, Honey was a lot more interested in Rhett than she was in him. He doesn't know it for certain, but he was pretty sure the two had hooked up at some point during the four-day weekend. I asked him about Honey's movements on the night Georgia died. Jedd said she claimed to have a headache and went up to their room shortly after dinner. He went up to check on her shortly after Georgia stormed out and Rhett went after her, but she wasn't in their room. When he asked her about it later, she said she'd taken a walk."

"So she was out on the grounds when Georgia was killed."

"Jedd believes so," Victoria answered.

"Does Jedd know where Honey is now?" I asked.

"No. They didn't stay in touch. Listen, I gotta go. My agent is waving at me. I can call you back in a couple of hours."

"Okay. Thanks for speaking to Jedd. I'll see if I can get you in to see Rhett. I might have a way to get around his team."

"Okay, but it will have to be tomorrow. I leave on Saturday."

"I'll see what I can do," I promised.

After I hung up with Victoria, I called Alex and left a message, asking him to see if Hillary could help them get Victoria in to see Rhett. I knew they were divorced, but I suspected she still had some pull with his people. If that didn't work, maybe Savage could find a legal way in.

Then I called Claudia and asked if she had a few minutes to chat. She was free and more than happy to answer any additional questions, so I told Clara where I was going and headed to the wealthy part of town. As she had before, Claudia met me at the door and escorted me to the living room, where she had hot tea waiting.

"Thanks for seeing me," I began. "I only have a few additional questions."

She nodded and waited for me to begin.

"I recently learned Dru Breland wasn't murdered on the same night as Georgia but in fact has only been dead about a year."

Claudia frowned. "A year?"

"It seems, based on the information I have, he'd been in hiding but returned to Gull Island around the time his brother sold the estate. I assume it was to retrieve something. I'm uncertain who might have known he was here, but I figured as the nearest neighbor you may have seen someone on the estate or noticed a car in the area."

"I'm afraid I can't help you with that. The last time I remember seeing any sign that the estate was occupied was five years ago. It's been completely deserted since the investigation into Georgia's death was completed and the family and guests all left."

"What about the moving crew?"

Claudia narrowed her gaze. "I imagine they must have been there while I was visiting my sister. I was away for over a month."

I paused while I formulated my next question. I didn't want to take up too much of Claudia's time, but I had hoped she had some insight into some of the points that were left hanging. "Jack and I spoke to Trent. He made a few comments that seemed inconsistent with what others have told us. Do you remember if you were with him at the time Wylie informed the Crawfords he'd found Georgia's body?"

"No. Trent wandered off at some point. I seem to remember I was speaking with Tiffany when we received the news of Georgia's death."

"Did you see Trent at the house later that evening?"

"Things became hectic once the sheriff's men arrived, but I'm sure he was around somewhere. I seem to remember hearing that everyone other than Dru was available to be interviewed, although I didn't stay around. As soon as I was cleared to leave, I walked home via the beach. I think Trent may have left by then, but I can't be sure. He was pretty drunk, so it could be that someone gave him a ride home. I'm sorry I can't be more help."

"Trent said he went to a bar in town and went home from there. He was interviewed the following day by a deputy who came to his home."

Claudia frowned. "I suppose that's possible. As I said, it was hectic and I went home as soon as I could. It seems there were several people out of the room when the deputies first showed up."

"And I think you mentioned you didn't stay in touch with Trent after the party."

Claudia shook her head. "We didn't have a lot in common. I needed a date for the party and he was willing to go; that was the extent of our relationship."

I glanced at the clock on the wall and realized I needed to get going if I wasn't going to be late to the Mystery Mastermind meeting. "I have somewhere I need to be, but I want to thank you again for your time. It really helps to get everyone's perspective. If you think of anything else, please do call me."

"Of course."

I thought about mentioning the body in the trunk on the off chance Claudia might know who the skeleton had once been, but for some reason instinct cautioned me to hold off sharing that piece of news. I had no reason not to trust Claudia, but the information we'd been receiving lately was becoming varied enough that I found myself suddenly suspecting everyone of something, including this neighbor, who seemingly had nothing to hide.

I was halfway home when Savage called. I pulled over to the side of the road to speak to him.

"You said you had news?" he asked.

I filled him in on my conversation with Trent. "I hoped you had access to the original sheriff's report. I'd be interested in knowing exactly what he told whoever interviewed him."

"Hang on; I can pull it up on the computer."

I waited while Savage accessed the report. He must have put me on speakerphone; I could hear him rustling papers and keyboarding.

"The report is very brief. It simply states that Trent Truitt was very hung over at the time of the interview and didn't seem to remember anything about the night before. The deputy made a note about following up at another time, but I haven't found any evidence he ever did."

"That does line up with what Trent told us. He said he was hammered the night of the party and extremely hung over the next day. He did seem to remember quite a bit about his movements during the night of the party when Jack and I spoke to him, though. Do you think it's possible he didn't remember anything the next day, but things came back to him later?"

"Extremely possible. I had that experience myself a time or two when I was younger."

"So do you think it's possible Trent and Dru really were in town drinking when Georgia was killed?"

Savage paused. "It seems to me that if Dru hadn't killed Georgia, he would have returned to the estate when he sobered up."

"That's what I thought too."

"And we still don't know where he was in the four years between Georgia's death and his own."

"It really does seem he must have been in hiding."

"I need to speak to Rhett," Savage said in a voice that conveyed his conviction. "I'm going to try to get hold of him again. Maybe I can use some of my LA connections. It seems to me he may be the one holding the pieces we need to make sense of this whole thing."

Chapter 12

Once everyone had gathered for the Mystery Mastermind meeting, I began by filling them in on the body we'd found in the trunk and what we knew—or, more importantly, didn't know— about it.

"The victim was a female in her late twenties. The cause of death hasn't yet been determined, but nothing obvious such as a gunshot wound has been found. Deputy Savage hasn't been able to find a missing persons report that would correlate to the victim, nor has he had any luck identifying the victim through dental records. Of course, that works best if you have an idea who the victim might be and use medical or dental records to confirm it."

"We know the woman had long dark hair and blue eyes," Clara added.

The others looked at me. "Clara had a vision of a third victim prior to our finding the body. In her vision, the woman had dark hair and blue eyes. I'm waiting for a call back from either Alex or Hillary. We're hoping to find out whether Hillary knows the identity of the woman."

"I did a search for old newspaper articles relating to a missing person at some point before Georgia Darcy's death but haven't come up with anything," Jack added. "I plan to broaden my search tomorrow."

"If the trunk belonged to Dru, and Rhett and Hillary both knew about it, it stands to reason they would have information that would help narrow things down," George pointed out. "I know Victoria hasn't had much luck getting through to Rhett, but surely Deputy Savage would be more successful."

"It would seem that would be the case, but as of the last time I spoke to him, he hadn't gotten through to Rhett either. He did seem determined to speak to him one way or another, though. I'm hoping Alex will have better luck with Hillary. She agreed to speak to him the first time, and she's the one who told us about the trunk in the first place, which says to me that she isn't trying to hide anything."

"It feels like we're obtaining new information but aren't really narrowing things down," Brit said.

"I agree. It does feel that way, but Jack and I talked about it, and we've put the eleven suspects on three lists. On list A are the people we feel most strongly could have killed Georgia. So far, we have Dru, Rhett, Wylie, and Trent."

"Why Trent?" Brit asked.

"It appears he lied to us about being with Dru during the time when Georgia was murdered."

"Lied how?" Brit asked.

I explained the bar story and the conflicting details.

"Okay, who else?" George asked.

"On the second list—I'm calling this list B—we have those who might have killed Georgia but aren't as strong suspects. That includes Hillary, Jedd, and Honey."

"Why Honey?" Brit asked.

I explained her departure from the party and seeming interest in Rhett.

"So that leaves Olivia, Tiffany, Claudia, and Reggie on the C list, the one for those who seem the least likely to have killed Georgia," Brit provided.

"Exactly. Jack and I didn't get the vibe that any of them had a motive, so unless any of you have new information, we've all but cleared them. At least for Georgia's murder. I suppose we need to look at Dru's murder separately."

Everyone took a moment to let that information sink in. I used a clean whiteboard to record the three lists.

"I'd like to ask the group if anyone has uncovered any information that would move any of these individuals from one list to another," I eventually said.

"I've been stalking Honey Golden on social media for the past few days, and while I haven't had the chance to interview her, I haven't seen anything that would indicate to me that she's hiding a secret as huge as a murder," Brit volunteered. "Additionally, according to what Jill learned, Honey had never been to the estate prior to that weekend. I'm not sure anyone has said where this toolshed Georgia was stuffed into was located, but chances are it was tucked away somewhere so it wasn't an eyesore. If that's true, it's unlikely Honey would even know where it was. And even if she was aware of its location, what possible motive could she have to kill Georgia? I get that Jedd suspected Honey had a thing for Rhett.

That's understandable. He is, and was, a famous, rich, handsome man. But she'd just met him. I don't buy that she'd see Rhett with Georgia and fly into a rage so intense that it would result in Georgia's death."

"Brit makes a good point," George added. "Although even if Honey didn't kill Georgia, she may have seen something." He looked at Brit. "Where are you with setting up an interview?"

"Honey is reluctant to discuss the matter, but I'll keep trying. I did have a bit of luck identifying the necklace Jill found."

I took a moment to fill everyone in on the necklace and where we found it.

"What did you find?" I asked Brit.

"A maker's mark. It's a signature of sorts. I tracked down the jeweler who'd used the mark but found they've been out of business for twenty years. The man who owned it and created the custom-made pieces passed away unexpectedly. I spoke to the man's son, who informed me that he still had many of his business's files. I forwarded a photo of the necklace and he agreed to see what he could find."

"So if he can find the paperwork we'll know who bought it originally?" I said.

"Exactly."

"Let us know right away when you hear back from the jeweler's son."

The room fell silent until my phone began to ring. "It's Alex," I informed the others before I answered. "Alex, I'm going to put you on speakerphone so everyone can hear what you have to say."

"That's fine."

I switched the phone over and then asked my first question. "Were you able to speak to Hillary again?"

"I was. She really is a very nice woman."

"I agree, she does seem nice. What did she have to say?"

"First of all," Alex began, "I want to make it clear that in my opinion there's no way this woman killed her sister. She seems to be genuinely grieved by her death. I did for a moment consider that she may have known Dru killed Georgia and that he was back in the States and could be responsible for his death, but after getting to know her, I seriously doubt that's true either."

"Okay. You have good instincts that I feel we can trust. Was Hillary able to provide you with any information that might lead to the person who did do the killings?"

"I'm not sure. I asked Hillary if she had any idea what was in the trunk and she swore she didn't. I told her there was a theory that the skeleton was of a woman in her twenties with dark hair and blue eyes, but she said that didn't ring a bell. She claimed not to have known anyone on the island until she met Tiffany. If the woman could have died as much as ten years ago, that would have been before Hillary and Tiffany met. Hillary did say it might not be a bad idea to ask Rhett about the woman because he spent a lot more time on the estate than she did. I mentioned we hadn't had any luck getting past his team and she just laughed and said she wasn't surprised. I asked if she could get Victoria in to see him and she promised to try, but she wasn't holding out much hope. When I explained exactly who Victoria was, though, her eyes got big and she said Rhett might agree to speak to someone who looked like her. I gave her Victoria's contact information so she can set up a meeting directly."

"That's great, Alex. Did Hillary know when the trunk first showed up on the estate?"

"She wasn't sure. She overheard Rhett and Dru arguing about it maybe seven years ago. At the time, she didn't understand the significance of the conversation because she had no idea what was in the trunk, but she did remember that Rhett wanted Dru to take it off the property and Dru refused. She isn't a hundred percent certain Rhett knew what was in it, but if he didn't know, she isn't sure why he would care if Dru kept it there. It was hidden away in a secret room in a wing of the house rarely used by anyone other than Dru."

"At this point we're operating under the assumption that Dru killed this woman, most likely on the property or at least on Gull Island, stashed her in the trunk, and then hid it in the secret room," I told Alex. "It appears this all happened shortly after Rhett bought the estate. Did Hillary say anything that would lead you to believe that couldn't be true?"

"No. Your theory makes sense. Hillary made it very clear Rhett had helped his brother out of sticky situations before. She said she wouldn't be surprised if he did know what was in the trunk. And she reiterated that it was her belief Dru killed Georgia and Rhett covered for him, though she doesn't have a clue who killed Dru."

"Thanks, Alex. This is all good information. Is there anything else you want to share?"

"Only that I'll be home tomorrow night. It'll be late, so I'll see everyone on Saturday."

"Vikki is coming home on Saturday too, and I'm planning to throw a casual party on the thirty-first."

"Great. I'll be there."

"Okay, who's next?" I asked after I hung up the phone.

"I'll go," George spoke up. "I have some information I only found out right before the meeting, but I want to talk about a few things I found out about the history of the house first. Some of it's just interesting, but I think some of it may turn out to be relevant."

"Okay. Go ahead," I encouraged.

"Although Clayton Powell owned and lived on the property we're referring to as the Crawford estate for four decades, not a lot is known about him. He's been credited with adding the north wing to the house as well as most, if not all, the secret passages and rooms. It seems he liked to be able to move around from one part of the house to another without being observed by anyone."

"But I thought you said he was a recluse who lived alone," Brit pointed out.

"He was," George confirmed. "I don't have an explanation for why he may have felt exposed while walking through the hallways of an empty house, but by all accounts, he built many of the passageways to avoid doing just that."

George picked up an old-looking book. "This is about mysterious buildings in the South. The Powell/Crawford house is mentioned. The author had the opportunity to tour it prior to Crawford purchasing it. There's no mention of rooms that led nowhere or steel-reinforced rooms. It's my opinion that after Rhett Crawford bought the house, he, or someone in his immediate circle, modified some of the passageways to suit their own needs."

"So Dru may have blocked off and reinforced a passage that originally led from one part of the house to another," I speculated.

"That would be my guess. The room off the wine cellar where Dru's body was found appears to have been altered as well. The home no longer exits and I assume many of the passages caved in when it was demolished, so it's hard to tell the extent to which Crawford altered things."

"Or why," Brit said.

I glanced at Jack, who had a frown on his face. I was beginning to think that both Dru Breland and his brother were sickos who might very well have been linked to the body in the trunk.

"You said you had other news?" I asked.

"Yes, and this is where things may get interesting, although, in fairness, it may also turn out to be completely irrelevant."

"Go on."

"After you told me about the body in the trunk, I attempted to find a missing person who would match it. I came up blank, like everyone else, but I did find a story about three women who went missing exactly two months apart eight years ago."

"Here?" I asked.

"No. In Los Angeles. I wouldn't have paid a bit of attention to the article I found, especially because the women disappeared on the other side of the country, but both Rhett and Dru lived in Los Angeles and the three women were all in their early twenties. Additionally, they all had long dark hair and blue eyes."

I sat forward. “Are you thinking either Rhett or Dru is a serial killer and the victim in the trunk was one of their victims?”

“It’s a long shot, yes. I forwarded the information to Deputy Savage, however. He called me back just as we were gathering tonight and informed me that he’d managed to get through to one of Rhett’s people, who informed him Rhett hadn’t been in Los Angeles for more than two weeks. He disappeared without a word, and no one, including his entire staff, knows where he is.”

“Maybe he’s here,” Brit exclaimed. “Maybe he knew the house was going to be demolished and he came to hide his bodies.”

“Maybe, but if that were true—and again, this is a long shot—why leave one to be found? For that matter, why leave Dru’s to be found?” George asked.

No one responded, I assumed because no one had an answer.

“I wonder why Savage didn’t mention that to me when I spoke to him earlier,” I said.

“He probably didn’t have this piece of information yet. As I said, he called me just as we were settling in.”

Brit spoke up. “I feel like we have three separate mysteries going on here that may or may not be related. First, there’s the murder of Georgia Darcy five years ago, then the murder of Dru Breland four years later, and then the murder of the woman in the trunk as much as ten years ago. If we look at each in isolation, we’re going to come up with completely different sets of suspects than if we look at them together.”

"Brit has a point," Jack jumped in. "It seems the only person who could have killed the girl in the trunk, Georgia, *and* Dru is Rhett, unless we want to consider Hillary."

"What about Jedd?" I asked. "He was also associated with Rhett and the estate, and if the missing girls in Los Angeles do turn out to be related, he was also living in LA when they went missing."

"Does anyone else feel like our decision to take a second look at Georgia Darcy's murder has turned into a big thing that's so far out of our league it's ridiculous?" Brit asked.

"It does seem things have escalated rather quickly," I agreed. "Does anyone want out?"

The room fell silent.

Eventually, Jack spoke up again. "I'm still in. If it does turn out that Rhett is some sort of psycho serial killer with a trail of bodies on both coasts, then yes, we're probably in over our heads. We'll just have to proceed carefully on that front. But it's still possible the answer could be as easy as Dru killing the girl in the trunk and Georgia in fits of rage, and then someone killing Dru when he returned to Gull Island to move the trunk."

"In that case, we just need to figure out who killed Dru," I added.

"Exactly. I think this may still be a difficult but not impossible task."

"I'm with you," I said to Jack.

"Yeah, me too." Brit nodded.

"I'm prepared to continue with my research," George joined in.

I glanced at Clara, who had yet to make a peep during the entire meeting. "Clara?"

"I'm not sensing a link between the woman in the trunk and the missing women in Los Angeles. My instinct is that the two cases aren't related. What I am sensing is a link between the skeleton in the trunk and Georgia Darcy. I don't think we should be distracted by murders or missing people beyond anything that occurred on the Crawford estate. The house, or the residents of the house, are the key to solving this mystery."

"Does that mean you're still in?" I clarified.

"I am, and so is Agatha."

I smiled as I glanced at the cat Clara was holding in her arms. Then I glanced at Blackbeard, who was watching us from his perch and who, likewise, had yet to utter a word. "Blackbeard? Are you in as well, buddy?"

"Secret kisses, secret kisses."

Somehow, I had the feeling secret kisses were going to end up being at the root of everything.

Chapter 13

Saturday, October 28

I woke up early to take a quick walk before I had to get ready to head over to the harvest festival. I was looking forward to working the kiddie carnival with Jack. I'd never done anything quite like it before, but I could remember always wanting to go to one when I was a kid. My mom had never found the time to take me, but maybe now I could enjoy the fun as an adult.

Alex had gotten in late the night before, as he'd said he would. I didn't want to wake him, so I figured we could catch up later in the day. There hadn't been any new developments in the case the previous day, but the gang had agreed to get together tonight to share any tidbits, however small, with the entire Mystery Mastermind group. Vikki was supposed to be home by midafternoon and I hoped she'd be available to meet with us as well. My plan for the day was to enjoy the festival while keeping my eyes and ears open for any clues I might pick up while surrounded by most of the island's residents.

I also wanted to touch base with Deputy Savage. I knew he was investigating all three murders on his own front, and it was entirely possible he'd uncovered something we hadn't. He did, after all, have resources available to him that we mere civilians didn't. If nothing else, I hoped he'd made progress on identifying the skeleton in the trunk. It seemed to me that figuring out who she was, how she'd gotten there, and why no one had ever moved her, might be the key to figuring out everything.

It was a crisp day, and the shorter and cooler nights had gone a long way toward changing the remaining deciduous trees to shades of bright orange, yellow, and red. After a long, hot shower, I dressed in a soft sweater in a light camel color, dark brown jeans, and dark brown leather boots that came to just below my knee. I applied a light dusting of makeup and deemed myself ready for whatever the day might bring. I made sure Blackbeard had plenty of fresh food and water, said good-bye to Clara, and headed to the recreation complex where the harvest festival was being held.

"Thank you so much for coming," Meg greeted me as I arrived at the area where the volunteers received their assignments. "I have both you and Jack at the dart game. He went on ahead to start blowing up the balloons."

"We have to blow up balloons?"

"Don't worry; we have a helium tank. The dart booth is five booths down in the second row. If you run out of balloons or anything, just give me a shout and I'll bring you whatever you need."

I looked out over the crowd. "Half the population of the island must already be here."

"It's a popular event, so we generally have a good turnout."

I took the packet Meg handed me, wondering where Brooke Johnson, the volunteer coordinator, was, though I supposed she could be organizing folks at either the food court or the craft fair.

"Let me know if you run into any problems," Meg added.

"Thank you. I'll go find Jack."

The busy energy of the kiddie carnival was electrifying. Music blared as kids of all ages ran up and down the aisles, stopping to play the games that most appealed to them. Based on the number of booths set up, I figured there must be at least thirty different games of varying skill levels to choose from. I wandered up and down each row, watching kids try out their skills. Once again, I found myself wishing I'd had the opportunity to attend an event like this when I was a kid. It seemed like everyone was having a wonderful time, and many of the games were beckoning me to give them a try. I was thinking of trying a few when my volunteer duty was over, though I didn't see many adults playing the games. I didn't suppose there was a rule against it.

"You made it," Jack greeted me with a smile.

I looked at the long line already assembled in front of the dart booth and realized I should have made my way to the booth more quickly. "I was talking to Meg, but I'm here now. What do you want me to do?"

"Each kid gets three darts for one blue ticket. And they get a red ticket for each balloon they pop. They can collect red tickets all day and then exchange them for prizes at the end. If someone wants to take more than one turn, they can, but they have to go to the end of the line after each try. If you want to handle the tickets, I'll make sure we have enough balloons to keep the board full for every new participant."

"Sounds easy enough." I let myself into the area behind the counter and greeted the first kid. I accepted his blue ticket, putting it in the bucket Jack had pointed out. The boy popped two balloons with his three darts and I gave him two red tickets. Then I accepted a blue ticket from the next kid while Jack replaced the two popped balloons with new ones from the pile he'd blown up. No problem, right?

Not at first.

"I popped three balloons and you only gave me two tickets," a boy with long hair that fell across his eyes and looked to be about ten complained.

"No. You only popped two balloons."

"Look again, lady. I had three darts and I popped three balloons."

Unfortunately, Jack had already cleared the popped balloons, so I couldn't prove how many had been popped one way or the other. I looked at Jack. "How many balloons were popped in the last round?"

"Two."

I glanced at the boy.

"You both need glasses. It was three." The boy looked at the kid standing next to him.

"I saw three popped balloons," he said in response to his buddy's prompt.

"Just give him three tickets," Jack finally said.

"Hey, that's not fair," the girl standing behind the boy doing the complaining said. "If he gets a free ticket, I want one too."

"Yeah, me too," about ten other kids chimed in.

"No one is getting extra tickets," Jack finally jumped in. "From now on, I won't remove the popped balloons until the red tickets are distributed, but keep in mind this is going to slow things down."

"But this is already the longest line," a girl toward the back whined.

That was the way most of the rest of our two-hour shift went. I guess once one kid starts in, they create a force that no mere adult can deal with.

"I knew there was a reason I never wanted to have kids," I complained after our two hours of hell finally came to an end.

"I actually used to think I might want a couple someday, but now I'm not so sure. Who knew kids could be so mean?"

"Right! Although I didn't notice the other volunteers having the problems we were. I think the kids realized we were rookies and took advantage. Once they got started, they were like piranhas in a feeding frenzy."

"So now that we've survived our initiation, what do you want to do?" Jack asked. "I seem to remember something about a free hot dog."

"I am hungry."

"I think the food court is this way." Jack took my hand and led me through the throngs of vultures who were waiting for their next kiddie-carnival virgin to torture.

The lines at the food court were even longer than the ones at the games, so after a bit of discussion Jack and I headed into town to grab a bite to eat there. Normally, the island restaurants would be crowded on a Saturday at lunchtime, but because almost everyone was at the harvest festival, we were able to walk right in and get a table by the window. We ordered and settled in to enjoy the beauty of a perfect autumn day.

"Did Alex make it home okay?" Jack asked.

"Yeah; his car is parked outside his cabin. He got in late, so I haven't spoken to him, but I know he plans to meet with us tonight, so we can catch up with him then. Vikki should be back as well. You should plan to come for dinner. Clara was making a huge pot of soup when I left this morning. It smelled wonderful."

"Homemade soup sounds a lot better than a microwave dinner."

"You seriously eat microwave dinners?"

Jack nodded. "When I'm home alone."

"You're rich. You should hire a cook."

"Maybe. For now, frozen dinners are fine. Did you ever figure out the recipe you were working on for the enchilada sauce you were trying to duplicate?"

"Sort of. After more than ten batches, I finally hit on a combination of ingredients that taste like the original. You'll have to come over for dinner next week and we can try it out."

"We still on for dinner on Tuesday?"

"We are, and I'm very excited to be hosting my first-ever Halloween dinner party, or any party, for that matter."

Jack looked surprised. "You've never thrown a party?"

"Never. When I was a kid, my mom didn't think kids and parties went together, so I never had a birthday party or any party, really, and once I moved out, I lived in a series of teeny-tiny apartments. To be honest, I worked a lot and didn't attend many parties either. But now I have friends and a surrogate family, and I'm ready to get wild and crazy."

Jack raised a single brow.

"Okay, maybe not wild and crazy, but I do see fondue in our future, and that's pretty wild."

Jack laughed. "I can't wait for your party. Should I bring something?"

"Wine? The good stuff."

"Done. Now we just need to get this murder mystery wrapped up before Tuesday so that won't interfere in any way."

"Do you have any new and exciting news to share on that front?" I asked.

"New, yes; exciting, not really."

"So share."

Jack leaned back in the booth before he began. "I was doing some research yesterday on another piece I'm working on and ran across an article written by the guy who owned the paper before me. I hadn't noticed it when I'd looked for information relating to Georgia Darcy's death because this was about murders in the area in general, not that murder specifically. The article didn't have any information we don't already know, but it did lead me to other articles about Georgia Darcy. I realized we'd been so focused on her death, we didn't really look in to her life."

"I guess that's true. What did you find?"

"For one thing, I found a photo. Georgia had long dark hair and blue eyes."

"Just like the others."

Jack nodded. “I think it’s important we don’t read too much into it, though. A lot of people have the same coloring, but I did find it interesting. I also find it interesting that Hillary has blond hair and green eyes. Sisters can have different coloring, but the two women don’t look anything alike, so I did a little digging, and it turned out Hillary and Georgia were half sisters. They shared a mother, whom both were estranged from at the time of Georgia’s death, but had different fathers.”

“I guess that’s interesting, but is it relevant?”

“Not necessarily. I just thought it was interesting and decided to bring it up. I also found out Hillary wasn’t Rhett’s first wife. It seems he was married when he was just nineteen to a woman he met while they were in high school. This was when he was a wannabe actor, living in a small town in Northern California, before he moved to Los Angeles and became a movie star. I found a photo of the first wife in an old high school yearbook and she also had long dark hair and blue eyes.”

“Was she murdered too?”

“Yes, but not by Rhett. She was stabbed to death in their home while Rhett was in Los Angeles, auditioning for a minor role in what would have been his first movie.”

I let that sink in. “So, are we back to the Rhett-as-a-serial-killer theory? It fits. Someone murders his first wife while he’s away from home and therefore unable to save her, so he begins picking up and murdering women with similar coloring as some sort of twisted revenge.”

“I think we need to be careful in making that leap. While the coincidences are beginning to pile up,

Hillary has completely different coloring and he married her, which would indicate he isn't totally fixated on dark-haired women with blue eyes."

"Unless she was his safe wife: a person he could share a life with and build a career with but not become obsessed with."

Jack shrugged. "Maybe. As I said, I found the coincidences interesting, but I think it would be a mistake to abandon our investigation in favor of putting all our marbles in that particular bag."

"Have you mentioned all this to Deputy Savage?"

"I called him last night and filled him in on everything I'd found. He said he'd follow up on it, and he told me he was in contact with a detective in LA who had investigated the missing women; they're comparing notes, just in case. Additionally, he informed me that an old buddy of his who's now in the FBI working out of their Los Angeles office agreed to have a chat with Rhett in an official capacity."

"I thought Rhett was missing," I said.

"He was, but he showed up at the studio yesterday for a viewing of the final edits on the film he has coming out soon. Savage's FBI friend met him there and they spoke. As of last night, Savage wasn't certain how that went."

"You know, it's beginning to feel like Deputy Savage is coming around to the idea of us as allies. He certainly seems to be a bit more open about sharing information than he was in the past."

Jack took a sip of his water. "I agree. Of course, he begins everything he says with the words *off the record*, but I understand why he would do that. Not that I would print anything that would be damaging to the case, but there are reporters who would."

The conversation paused when the waitress brought our meals. We ate in silence until a good portion of the food had been demolished.

"I guess we were hungry." Jack laughed as I wiped my plate with the last of the crust from my sandwich.

"Being eaten alive by a group of elementary-school kids will do that to you."

"Do you have plans for the rest of the afternoon?" Jack asked.

"I need to run a few errands and then I thought I'd head home to see if Vikki's there yet. I can't wait to hear all about her movie deal. How about you?"

"I have an article to write."

"But you'll be by this evening?"

"I will. Say six?"

"Six is good. I'm looking forward to Clara's soup."

We finished our meal, paid the bill, and walked out to the lot where we'd parked. We were saying our good-byes when Jack's phone rang.

"Jack Jones."

I watched as he listened to the person on the other end. Eventually, he spoke. "Jill and I are just down the street. How about if we stop by?"

I realized he must be speaking to Savage.

"Okay; we'll be there in a few minutes." Jack hung up.

"Does he have news?"

"He said he does. Do you have time to stop by?"

"I'll make time."

Savage was waiting for us in the reception area when we arrived. He escorted us into his office and motioned for us to take seats on the far side of his desk.

"You have news?" I jumped in.

He nodded. Then he looked at Jack. "This is off the record."

"Agreed."

"My friend at the FBI had a sit-down with Rhett Crawford and his high-priced attorney. He was willing to share what he knew in exchange for immunity from any charges relating to the case. He also made it part of the deal that his name wasn't to be linked to the case in any public records or statements."

I supposed that made sense. He certainly wouldn't want to do anything that would have a negative impact on his career.

"And did they make a deal?"

"Yes."

"And…?" I asked anxiously.

"And it turns out that, as we all have, Rhett suspected Dru was responsible for Georgia's death, though he claims not to have had firsthand proof of it until recently. He knew Dru left the party in a hurry and basically dropped out of sight. He didn't know what had become of his brother until about two years ago, when he received a call from Dru from out of the blue. Dru didn't tell him where he was, but he did say he'd undergone a life-altering experience that made him want to begin to make things right. During that conversation, Dru confessed to Rhett that he and Georgia had argued, the argument had become physical, he'd pushed Georgia, and she'd fallen and hit her head. He said he'd tried to save her by giving her CPR but was unsuccessful. He panicked and hid her body in the toolshed, figuring no one would find her until he'd had the chance to get away. Trent was sitting in the yard, drinking whiskey, and he paid him twenty-five-thousand dollars to drive him to his buddy's house up north, where he arranged to disappear."

"He must have worked out a lie for Trent to tell should he be questioned about it," I said.

"That would seem to be the case," Savage agreed.

"And the body in the trunk?"

"Rhett claims not to have known anything about that. He thought Dru kept a stash of drugs in there; his brother had a problem with drugs. He seemed as surprised as anyone to find out the trunk held a body. He told the FBI he had no idea who the skeleton may have been."

I wasn't entirely sure I believed Rhett didn't know what was in the trunk, but if he'd already worked out immunity, I wasn't sure why he'd lie.

"So we know Dru killed Georgia, but we still don't know who killed Dru or anything about the body in the trunk," Jack summarized.

"Exactly," Savage confirmed.

We went out to our individual cars and Jack drove away, while I was about to start mine when Brit called.

"The jeweler's son called back," she said.

"And…?"

"And he found the name of the person who bought the necklace."

"And…?" I asked a bit more impatiently.

"And the woman who bought the custom-made piece was named Lorraine Norris."

I frowned. "As in Claudia Norris?"

"Lorraine was her grandmother. She passed away eleven years ago."

I remembered Claudia had lived in her big house with her sister, Madison, until they had a falling-out over an inheritance from their grandmother. And that Claudia had been away visiting her sister when the movers had cleaned out the Crawford home, so it appeared they'd reconciled. Claudia had visited the Crawford estate on occasion. She'd admitted to spending time with Georgia. If she had been wearing her grandmother's necklace, she could have dropped it at some point.

"Thanks, Brit. I need to speak to Claudia about something else anyway. I'll run by the resort to pick up the necklace. I can return it to her when I drop by."

"I'm on my way out. I'll leave it on the little table next to the front door of the main house."

After I hung up, I drove out to the resort, picked up the necklace, and then headed over to Claudia's. Even with Dru's confession to Rhett that he was the one who'd killed Georgia, I couldn't get the mystery of the woman in the trunk out of my head. Claudia had lived next door to the estate where the body was discovered for a lot of years. Even if a woman with dark hair and blue eyes didn't come to mind right away, another discussion about things that had occurred on the island years before might jog her memory.

Chapter 14

Claudia answered the door on the first knock. She had to have been standing directly on the other side of it for her to have answered so quickly. I wondered if she'd been on her way out.

"Jill. What are you doing here?"

"I was at the Crawford estate the other day, trying to catch my bird, Blackbeard, who'd escaped, and I found this." I held out the necklace. "I did some research and found out it originally belonged to your grandmother, so I figured you must have lost it when you were visiting."

Claudia frowned, but then quickly smiled. She held out a hand. "Thank you so much. I've been wondering where I could have lost this. It's one of my favorites."

"I'm glad I could return it. There's something else too, if you have a few minutes."

Claudia hesitated, then opened the door wider. "Sure. I was about to go out, but I guess I have a few minutes. Let's go back to the living room."

I followed Claudia down the hallway. It was strange; she had a smile on her face, but she seemed nervous.

"How can I help you?" Claudia asked after sitting down across from me.

"You know Jack Jones and I have been looking in to the deaths of Georgia Darcy and Dru Breland."

"Yes, you mentioned it when you were here the other day. Have you found something out?"

I knew I couldn't discuss what I knew about Georgia's killer, so I skipped over that completely. "We haven't identified Dru's killer, but we found a third body."

Claudia's eyes narrowed. "A third body?"

"In a trunk in a secret room. The really odd thing is…" I paused when my phone beeped, letting me know I had a text. I glanced at it. It was from Jack. He'd sent a photo of a beautiful young woman with long dark hair and blue eyes wearing the necklace I'd just handed Claudia. Below the photo, Jack had typed, *The body in the trunk was Claudia's sister, Madison Norris.*

I paled and looked up at Claudia.

"You were saying…" she encouraged.

"It was your sister. The body in the trunk was your sister. Did you know? Did Rhett kill her?"

"Rhett? Why would Rhett kill her?"

"Because of his obsession with his first wife."

"What obsession?"

I remembered Claudia had told me that she'd been visiting her sister when the movers came to clear out the Crawford estate, and that I'd found in earlier research that Claudia had only one sister.

"You knew. You knew Rhett, or maybe Dru, had killed your sister." Suddenly a light went on. "It was Dru. You figured it out and killed him when he returned for the trunk."

I stared at Claudia. Her face had grown hard, but she didn't answer.

"But why would Dru kill your sister?" I demanded.

Claudia still didn't answer.

I looked directly into her eyes. There was so much rage there. "He didn't kill Madison, did he?" Oh God; I knew what had happened. "You did. He just helped you hide the body."

Claudia stood up and took a step toward me. "You're a stupid, stupid woman to have come here the way you did."

She had a point. What exactly was my strategy in confronting a woman with whom I was alone in her own home? Maybe I should have made an excuse to leave when I'd received Jack's text, although, based on the look on Claudia's face, I doubted she would have let me go even before I spilled my guts.

"Why did you kill your sister?" I found myself asking, almost against my will.

"She stole what should have been mine."

I waited.

"My grandmother, devil woman she was, was quite ill for the last five years of her life. She needed constant care but refused to go into a home, so I was forced to give up my life to take care of her while Princess Madison was free to go about her life."

"That must have been difficult."

"It was. Madison would pop in every week or two and spread sunshine and joy around the place.

Grandmother loved her almost as much as she hated me."

"She hated you? Why?"

"The woman was very ill. She required constant care. Much of it was painful or degrading, and she blamed me for all if it. I was only doing what the doctors assured me I had to do, but when she looked at me, all she could see was the living embodiment of the hell she was going through. After she died, I found out she'd left everything to Madison. I assumed Maddie would be reasonable and agree to share her inheritance with me, but she didn't. She was going to kick me out of my own home."

"I thought the two of you lived here together."

"We did for a while, but then Maddie decided she wanted to sell the house so she could move to Paris and pretend to be a painter. We fought, and she fell down the stairs. Dru and I were seeing each other at the time. He knew my situation and was sympathetic. He stopped by before I could figure out what to do with the body and helped me come up with a plan. It was a good one too. I told everyone Madison and I had had a falling-out and she went to Paris. She'd been telling everyone she was moving there for months, so no one questioned it. I was safe. No one would find out. And then Dru found religion and everything began to fall apart."

"So you killed him."

"I had to. All I wanted to do was move the dang body, but it seemed he'd grown a conscience since I'd seen him last. He threatened to tell Sheriff Bowman what he knew."

"So you stabbed him and tossed him in the hidden room."

Claudia didn't respond, but I could see it was true.

"Why didn't you move Madison's body yourself after Dru was dead?" Obviously, she hadn't, because we'd found it.

"I tried to get Dru to open the door to the underground vault where I knew he'd hidden it, but he knew I planned to dump Madison in the ocean and refused. I thought I could get in on my own, but the door was too sturdy and I couldn't figure out the combination. How'd you get it open?"

"Explosives."

"Oh. Yes, that would have worked. I'm sorry I didn't think of it. Of course, I figured once the trunk was found everyone would assume Dru was the one who'd killed Madison and he was dead, so he couldn't deny it. I thought I was safe, and I would have been if you hadn't come snooping around. I should have killed you when I first found out what you were up to."

"Are you going to kill me now?"

"I guess I'm going to have to. You've left me little choice."

"You always have a choice."

Claudia glanced at the front door. "I really do need to go, and your presence presents a dilemma."

I stood up. "Then I'll be on my way."

"Nice try." Claudia walked across the room. She approached an antique desk and opened a drawer. I gasped when she pulled out a small gun.

"You're going to shoot me?"

"Too messy."

"So you're going to let me go?"

"Sorry. It's way too late for that." Claudia pointed the gun toward the hallway. "Walk."

I had no choice but to obey and fought the urge to pass out as I stumbled my way down the hall. The hallway led to stairs down to the cellar. On the far side of that was a doorway. Claudia opened the door and motioned me inside. It seemed she had a secret room of her own. She slammed the door and the room plunged into darkness.

Suddenly, I really, really regretted my rash decision to confront this obviously unstable woman. I had my phone, which I pulled out of my pocket, but I wasn't able to make a call in the dark room, though I could use the flashlight on it to look around.

The good news was that the room didn't appear to be airtight. Unlike Dru's steel-reinforced vault, this room seemed to simply have been sectioned off from the rest of the cellar and constructed from two-by-fours and sheets of plywood. If given enough time, I could probably find a way to break out.

The room was mostly empty except for a pile of boxes stacked on the far wall. I walked over to them and opened the lid of one of the boxes on the top. It was filled with photos and other mementos of someone's life. I picked up a photo dated thirty years earlier that showed two young girls with their arms around each other, laughing at something as they looked into the camera. They were most likely Claudia and Madison. How had they gotten from being friends sharing a giggle to sisters cheating and killing each other?

The entire thing made me sad, so I closed the lid and set the box aside. I hoped I'd find something in one of the boxes to help me escape, but all I found were photos, old books, clothing, and various household knickknacks.

I looked at my phone again. Still no service. I wasn't thrilled to have been left in the chilly, dark room, but Brit knew where I was heading and I suspected Jack would try to track me down when he realized I'd never responded to his text. Of course, I had no way of knowing how long Claudia would be gone or what she planned to do with me when she returned. Perhaps I should try to find a way out instead of looking through old boxes of someone else's mementos.

The walls were made of wood and wood products, but I couldn't punch my way through them. I'd tried the door several times, but it was locked tight. I hadn't found any sharp objects capable of cutting through the wood or anything heavy enough to use to smash my way out.

I had learned how to unhinge a door during the remodel I was overseeing. Of course, I would still need some basic tools I didn't have. The floor was made of large pieces of plywood that I might be able to work loose, although chances were there was nothing but dirt beneath. But most, if not all, of the homes this close to the water had been built on piers, so there was a good chance if I could pry loose a piece of wood I could slip out through the bottom and then escape onto the beach.

I didn't have another plan, so I fell to my hands and knees and used my flashlight to begin looking for a loose board I could pry off. It took a while, but I managed to find a warped board that was already lifting in one corner. Now all I needed was something to pry beneath it. One of the boxes I'd noticed held kitchen utensils. I wasn't sure whether they'd just bend under the force of trying to lift the board, but I had nothing to lose by trying, so I chose the sturdiest pieces I could find and began working at the nails that secured the wood. I was making some progress when I heard someone on the other side of the door. I quickly grabbed a small kitchen knife and positioned myself just on the other side of the door. My best bet was to grab Claudia the minute she stepped inside. I figured she'd be temporarily blinded by the darkness. I just hoped she wouldn't shoot me before I could subdue her.

Once the door opened everything happened quickly. I jumped on the back of the person who walked into the room and stabbed my little knife against the fleshy part of my victim's neck. The next thing I knew, I was being flipped over the head of the person I'd tried to overcome, landing hard on my back.

A flash of light blinded me. I put a hand over my eyes.

"Jill?"

The voice wasn't that of a woman but a man. I slowly opened my eyes and tried to focus in the light. "Jack?"

"You stabbed me."

I cringed at the trail of blood running down his neck. "I'm sorry. I thought you were Claudia. She had a gun."

Jack wiped the blood from his neck, then put out a hand to help me up.

"Are you hurt bad?" I asked.

"It's just a scratch. The knife was dull and you're a bit of a weakling."

"I am not."

Jack just smiled. He took my hand and led me out of the room. Once we were on the other side of the door, I threw my arms around him and hugged him despite the fact that I was getting blood from his neck all over my sweater. "How did you know I was here?"

Jack squeezed me tightly before answering. I could feel the emotion in his hug. The poor guy seemed to really have been scared. "I called your cell when you didn't text me back and you didn't answer, so I called the house. When no one answered there, I called Brit, who told me where you'd gone. I knew you were still here because your car is in the drive. When no one answered my knock, I called Savage and then came in to look for you. I've been here for twenty minutes. Sorry it took so long to make my way down here."

"And Savage?"

"Upstairs. Claudia isn't here."

"We need to find her. She killed Dru and Madison."

"Don't worry; we'll find her. Savage has already put out an APB. I doubt she got far."

Chapter 15

Tuesday, October 31

"I'd like to make a toast." I held my glass high after everyone was seated for my first-ever holiday dinner party. "When I first agreed to come to Gull Island, I was in a pretty low place. I wasn't even sure I wanted to come here, but I felt like I needed a temporary place to regroup. I wasn't expecting to fall in love with the place, and I certainly wasn't expecting to find good friends who feel like family. I love you all and want to thank each and every one of you for making me feel like I have a real home, probably for the first time in my life."

"Hear, hear," they responded. "We love you too."

Once all the cheering had stopped, Jack stood up. "I too would like to thank everyone. Not only did you all contribute in a significant way to a story for the *Gull Island News* that could put us on the map, you helped to solve three murders and put a killer behind bars." Jack looked at Deputy Savage, who had managed to track down and arrest Claudia. "Of course, the article would have been a lot juicier if Rick hadn't insisted that everything be *off the record*."

Savage shrugged. I couldn't help but notice that not only was he sitting next to Victoria but she was glancing at him with a look I could only describe as longing. Maybe there was hope for those crazy kids after all.

"And let's not forget the role Mortie played," Gertie, who was sitting between George and Clara, added. "If not for Mortie's insight about the body in the secret room, this whole thing might never have gotten started."

"To Mortie," I said, holding up my glass once again.

I glanced at Blackbeard. "Do you have anything to add?"

"Secret kisses, secret kisses."

"Did you ever find out what that was all about?" Brit asked.

"Not really, though there did seem to be a lot of secret kissing going on. I found out Claudia had a thing going on with Dru at the time she killed Madison, which is why he agreed to help her hide her body. And we know Rhett was sleeping with Georgia, who was also sleeping with Dru." I glanced at Savage. "Did you ever track down Wylie Slater?"

"I did. It seems he's been using the estate to woo women ever since it was abandoned five years ago. Although Rhett Crawford laid him off and Wylie bought the fishing boat to provide a source of income, Rhett let him live in the cabin until he sold the estate. Wylie wasn't satisfied with that. Because the house was just sitting there empty, he'd been living in the big house, playing rich guy to a parade of women until just recently, when he met his current girlfriend."

"Is that why he took off? He was afraid we'd find out he'd been living in the house without permission?" I asked.

"He didn't take off. Not in the way we imagined anyway. He just decided to take his girlfriend up the coast to see her mother."

I guess everyone had been right about him; he was a good guy after all. "Did you ever find out how he happened to find Georgia's body in the toolshed on the night of the party?"

"Someone puked in the pool. He couldn't find the skimmer, so he went to the shed to see if he could find something that would work."

"Ewww," everyone around the table moaned.

"I have to say, this really has been an interesting case," George added. "And I feel as if we've gained leads on other interesting cases as well."

Jack grinned. "You're thinking about Clayton Powell's murder. That grabbed my attention as well. Maybe we can look in to it for our next case."

"Actually," Alex interrupted, "I have a case I'd like to put before the group."

They all nodded for him to continue.

Alex looked at Rick Savage. "Anything I'm about to say is off the record. If you aren't comfortable with putting the sheriff thing aside for the duration of this discussion, I'll have to ask you to leave for a few minutes. If you want to stay as a friend, you're welcome to."

"Are you going to confess to a crime or reveal one someone else committed?"

"No, not directly. What I'm about to talk about is public record, although it's a bit sensitive because I'm going to suggest that a law enforcement official may not have done their job the way they should have."

Savage nodded. "I can live with that. I agree to participate in this conversation as a friend, not a deputy."

"Okay, great." Alex took a deep breath, then began. "Trey Alderman is probably Gull Island's most important claim to sports fame. He was the starting pitcher for the Gull Island Seagulls, who went on to stand out nationally among college players while attending the University of South Carolina. It was assumed he would be a top draft pick a year and a half ago, and it seemed the sky was the limit for him. Trey came home on spring break during his senior year and, while on the island, agreed to play in a charity game held in Charleston. The game, which featured other draft hopefuls, was close and, in fact, had he hit even a single, he would have been responsible for the winning run. It was the bottom of the ninth, bases loaded, two outs, full count, and the tension was high. The pitch was thrown, everyone in the crowd held their breath, and Trey swung the bat with all his might before falling to the ground."

"What?" Brit asked. "Why?"

"Heart attack. He was a strong, healthy twenty-two-year-old with no prior heart or medical conditions of any kind. It was later determined that he had a high quantity of a mix of drugs in his system that, when taken together, can cause a heart attack in certain situations, such as high stress. The drugs were all the sort commonly used recreationally, and Trey had been to a party the previous evening. His death was declared an accident."

"But you don't think so?" I said.

"I think there were circumstances that should have been considered that weren't taken into account." Alex looked at Savage. "The death occurred in Charleston, although Trey was staying on Gull Island at the time, and whether he willfully ingested the drugs or not, he most likely would have ingested them here on the island." Alex looked at Savage. "I know the Charleston PD investigated the incident, but I'm not sure how involved you were."

"I wasn't involved at all. Both the medical examiner and the sheriff's department determined Trey died as the result of a terrible accident. The family didn't pursue an investigation."

"You think he was murdered?" Victoria gasped.

"Maybe he was and maybe he wasn't. I'm not sure why this case interests me so much, but it does. I spoke to my agent while I was in New York about writing a book about Trey's life and death. I know I usually write science fiction, but I find I'm in the mood for a change of pace, and I can afford to take a chance on a book that might not sell as well as my other stuff."

"Have you spoken to his family?" George asked.

"Yes, I have. I agreed to give them a percentage of sales if the book is published. My agent is working on the contract. If everything goes well, I plan to make a trip to Philadelphia, where Trey's parents live now, within the next week or so. Once I interview them, I'll decide on an approach, but I'll tell you all upfront that what I'm really interested in is finding out what happened to Trey. I'd welcome all the help I can get from the group."

No one spoke as they looked around the room at one another. Finally, Jack broke the silence. "I'm in. It'll be a tough one, but I imagine many of the people who attended the party with Trey still live on the island and may provide us with a starting point."

"I'm in too," I seconded. "I don't know much about baseball, but I'm always up for a good mystery."

"I'm in too," Brit said.

"Ditto," Victoria said.

"I'll start researching it right away," George spoke up.

Alex looked at Clara. "Of course, dear. Anything you need, you just ask."

I noticed Savage hadn't said anything, but I imagined he wanted a chance to look at the case from the law enforcement perspective first.

"Okay." Alex smiled. "I should have something for us to discuss by our regular Monday meeting in two weeks."

"Fantastic," I said. "Although I may have a conflict on the 13th. Will Wednesday November 15th work?"

Everyone agreed that it would.

"Okay great let's plan on that. In the meantime, I'll go online to see what I can learn about baseball in general."

The others continued to chat about the upcoming case, but I noticed Savage get up and step outside to make a call. I waited until he was back and approached him. "Are you okay with this?"

"I'll let you know after I look in to things, but on the surface, yeah, I'm fine. It wasn't my case back then, but I'll admit to being curious about it."

"You have a scowl on your face. Is something else wrong?"

"I just received some news I was waiting for," he shared.

"I take it the news was upsetting?"

"Can you keep a secret?"

"Yes."

"I found out Sheriff Bowman is suffering from early onset dementia, which, I'm afraid, has been behind his faulty decision-making lately."

"Oh no. I'm so sorry."

"It's progressed rapidly, which is why he's seemed so forgetful. He can't remember what's going on or what he's already told people, so he just stalls."

"That does explain a lot."

"Sadly, it does. He's been relieved from his job and a new sheriff will be chosen in the next election. For now, Deputy Houston has been chosen to fill in."

"Deputy Houston? I don't think I've met him."

"He works out of the main office. He's an okay guy, but he can be rigid, and I understand he's running for sheriff, so chances are he's going to be a by-the-book guy. He'll want to avoid scandal. I'm telling you this so you can inform your little group that they're going to need to tread lightly."

"Yeah. Okay. I'll tell them."

Savage looked off into the distance. "I'm going to take off. Thank you for dinner. Will you please tell everyone good-bye?"

"I will." I placed my hand on his arm. "And I'm sorry."

Savage let out a breath. "Yeah. Me too."

I stood and watched him walk away, then looked back to the house, with the orange lights around the door and the jack-o'-lanterns in the window, and said a prayer of thanks for the people who had come into my life. There was a time I couldn't imagine having so many friends; now I couldn't imagine my life without them.

"Penny for your thoughts," Jack said as he joined me outdoors.

"I was just thinking how lucky I am to have so many amazing people in my life."

Jack put his arm around my shoulder and I put my head on his arm as we stood side by side, looking into the window.

"It does feel like you've created a family here," Jack agreed.

I smiled. "I never had much of a family. My dad left when I was just a baby and my mom was always fluttering around the globe. I didn't have siblings or even close friends. We moved around a lot, and I never did have a place that felt like home. Then I found out I had a half brother I never knew and moved to Gull Island, and now I have a home and friends and even surrogate parents in the form of George and Clara. Suddenly, my life feels full and complete. I don't know if I can leave it."

"Leave it? Are you planning to leave?"

I turned slightly so I could see Jack's face. He really was such a sweet, handsome man. "When I came to Gull Island it was going to be a temporary thing. I just needed somewhere to regroup while I worked to get my old life back."

"I do remember you saying that."

"I figured the process of rebuilding what I'd lost would take a while, years even, but I got a call from an editor who read my piece on the Friday the Thirteenth Massacre, and she offered me a job writing for a news magazine."

I felt Jack's arm tighten around me. "Is it a good offer?" he asked.

"It's a very good offer. A month or two ago I would have jumped at it." I smiled as I watched George and Brit waltzing to "Monster Mash" through the window.

"But now?" Jack asked.

I took a step away and faced him. He looked directly into my eyes. I'd just found out about the job offer and hadn't had a chance to think it through, but suddenly I knew. "But now my life is here. I hadn't decided what to do until this moment, but as I watched the people I've grown to love having so much fun, I realized the thing that's been missing from my life isn't a high-power career but a family."

Jack touched his hand to my cheek. I could sense he wanted to say something, but he hesitated. Instead, he leaned in and brushed my lips ever so gently with his own. I wasn't certain at that moment where our paths would take us, but I saw promise in his eyes, and I realized I'd been a fool to push him away when all I really wanted to do was find a home in his arms.

Coming next from Kathi Daley Books

Preorder today

Preview Chapter 1

Wednesday, November 15

Trey Alderman was Gull Island's most important claim to sports fame. He was the starting pitcher for the Gull Island Seagulls and went on to stand out nationally among college players while attending the University of South Carolina. It was assumed he would be a top draft pick a year and a half back, and it seemed the sky was the limit in terms of his career.

Trey came home on spring break during his senior year and, while on the island, agreed to play in a charity event in Charleston. The game, which featured other draft hopefuls, came down to a single run. It was the bottom of the ninth, the tying run was on third, the bases were loaded, there were two outs, and the tension was high. The pitch was thrown fast and down the middle and the crowd held their breath as Trey swung his bat with all his might before falling to the ground. He was pronounced dead at the scene. It was later determined he died of a heart attack. He was twenty-two, healthy, and, as far as anyone knew, had no preexisting heart condition.

It was later revealed that Trey had arrived at the game feeling dizzy and disoriented. He'd elected to suit up but wasn't in the starting lineup. He'd begun to feel better as the game progressed and by the ninth inning he was feeling amped and ready to play, so the coach put him in as a pinch hitter in the bottom of the ninth. The autopsy revealed that Trey didn't have an undiagnosed heart condition, as everyone had believed, but had been suffering the ill effects of a drug mixture in his system that could have led to a heart attack when combined with extreme stress. The local investigators determined that he had most likely engaged in recreational drug use at a party he'd attended the previous evening.

Alex Cole, a twenty-eight-year-old, fun and flirty millennial who'd made his first million writing science fiction when he was just twenty-two, had decided to write a book about Trey's life and death and had brought the mystery of Trey's death to the Mystery Mastermind group made up of people who lived and worked at the Gull Island Writers' Retreat, which my brother, Garrett Hanford owns, and I, Jillian Hanford, operate.

"On the surface, it seems as if Trey's death was the result of his own poor choices," I pointed out. "I guess my question is: where's the mystery?"

"There are those, including Trey's parents, who believe he didn't knowingly consume the drugs that led to his death," Alex answered.

"They think someone slipped him the drugs without his knowledge?" I clarified.

"Exactly. It's my intention to dig into the twenty-four hours leading up to his collapse and try to determine if Trey's death really was nothing more than a terrible accident or if he was murdered."

"You're suggesting whoever slipped Trey the drugs, if that's even what happened, knew they would cause his heart to fail?" I asked.

"Not necessarily. Trey's heart attack seems to have been the result of a very specific set of circumstances that couldn't have been planned or predicted, so my use of the word *murdered* is probably a bit more melodramatic than the situation warrants. Still, I do believe someone could have slipped Trey the drugs with the intention of making him ill enough that he'd miss the game."

"Have you had a chance to narrow down the lists of suspects and witnesses we need to follow up with?" Brit Baxter, a twenty-six-year-old chick lit writer and the newest member of our group asked.

"I have nine names I think should give us a starting point," Alex said as his long blond hair fell over his bright blue eyes. "Everyone on the list attended the same party Trey did the night before he died, all attended the game, and all had at least a somewhat of a motive for wanting Trey out of the way."

I grabbed a bright red marker and stood in front of whiteboard, prepared to take notes as the discussion unfolded. We'd found that writing everything down permitted us to look at situations from a variety of perspectives and, in the end, helped us make sense of what usually began as a lot of unrelated information.

"I'll start with the residents of Gull Island who attended the party," Alex began as the group listened intently. "Fortunately, four of these five people still live on the island and are willing to speak to us when we're ready to begin our investigation."

"You've already spoken to everyone on the list?" asked George Baxter, a sixty-eight-year-old writer of traditional whodunits.

"I've spoken very briefly to more than half the people on the list so far," Alex confirmed. "I figured it would save us some time if I did a bit of the legwork ahead of time."

"Okay," I said, marker in hand. "What do you have?"

"Heather Granger dated Trey Alderman all though high school. It was assumed Trey and she would marry at some point, and Heather had even applied to the University of South Carolina and sent in her acceptance there as soon she found out that was the school he'd decided on. Shortly after their high school graduation, Trey broke up with her. He offered the standard we're-entering-a-new-phase-in-our-lives speech and asked her if she wanted to consider attending one of the other schools where she'd been accepted to make things less awkward."

"What a creep," Brit said with a hint of disgust in her voice. "If he didn't want his old girlfriend to interfere with his groove, *he* should have changed schools."

"The University of South Carolina was Trey's choice in the first place," Alex pointed out. "Heather was only going there to follow him."

"Whatever." Brit rolled her eyes.

"So what did Heather decide to do?" I asked to prevent an all-out argument. "Did she change schools?"

"She didn't go to college at all. From what I understand, she was pretty broken up when Trey dumped her from out the blue, and most of the people I've spoken to said she sank into a bit of a depression. She has, however, gotten on with her life since then," Alex assured us, looking directly at Brit. "She's engaged to a chef she met just after Trey's death and they've bought that old storefront on the wharf and are opening a restaurant."

"If she's has moved on, why is she on your list?" Brit asked.

"Because she hadn't moved on at the time of the party. In fact, I've heard she was quite enraged when Trey showed up with his new girlfriend, Rena Madison."

"Tell us about Rena," Brit suggested.

Alex hesitated. "I'd planned to cover the locals first and then move on to the visitors to the island who attended the party."

"It's okay. I can hop back and forth between the two lists and I'd like to hear about Rena as well," I said encouragingly.

"Okay," Alex agreed, sorting through his notes. "Rena Madison was a popular cheerleader at the University of South Carolina. She started dating Trey when they were both juniors. From what I've been able to find out, she's both beautiful and popular, and while she was majoring in communication, she had big plans to make a name for herself in modeling. While she didn't say as much to me, based on what others have told me, Rena was using Trey to advance her career. I can't speak to what was actually in her heart, but Trey's best friend from high school, Hudson Dickerson, shared with me that Trey planned to dump Rena as soon as he was drafted, so in a way it appears they were using each other."

"Like I said, the guy was an ass." Brit's eyes flashed with annoyance. "Why are we trying to find out what happened to him again?"

"You're helping me write a book based on a set of circumstances I'm exploring. Trey Alderman may not be a sympathetic character, but I do find him an interesting one."

"Oh, right. Okay, continue."

I could see Trey's cavalier attitude toward the women he dated had become a sore spot for Brit. It would appear the blond-haired pixie was a lot more of a romantic than she let on.

"Do we have reason to believe Rena knew Trey planned to dump her?" asked Jackson Jones, a never-married, forty-two-year-old, nationally acclaimed author of hard-core mysteries and thrillers, who was as famous for his good looks and boyish charm as he was for the stories he penned. Jackson currently lived on Gull Island as mild-mannered Jack Jones, small-town newspaper owner.

"I spoke to a woman named Candy Baldwin. She was and still is Heather's best friend and has lived on the island all her life. She said Rena *did* know what Trey planned and had told everyone at the party she'd find a way to get her revenge."

"Do you have the sense Candy is someone whose word can be trusted?" Jack asked.

Alex shrugged "I'm not sure. She's a nice enough woman who's since married her own high school boyfriend, Hudson Dickerson."

"Trey's best friend?" I clarified.

"Yes. It seems all through high school Trey and Heather and Hudson and Candy weren't only best friends but best couple friends. It's been suggested to me that Candy took Trey's breakup with Heather and the end of their little group almost harder than Heather did. I can't say for certain yet, but it seems Candy might hold a pretty big grudge against the victim, so I guess I'd take anything she tells you with a grain of salt."

"Should Candy and Hudson both be added to the suspect list?" I wondered.

Alex shook his head. "I would definitely consider Candy a suspect at this point. Hudson was Trey's best friend; as far as I can tell, he didn't have a motive to want to hurt him, but he was at the party and the game, so at the very least he's a witness. Add him to the list of people we should follow up with."

I made a few notes on the whiteboard, then asked Alex to go on.

"There are two locals we haven't discussed yet," he said. "Dexter Parkway was a bit of a nerd in high school, went on to pursue a career in computer science, and is currently working on a doctorate at

Harvard. While in high school, he was an unpopular geek who saw Trey as something of a hero. Dexter idolized Trey and spent quite a lot of time not only following him around but doing his homework, while Trey treated him like a trained dog."

Brit didn't say a word, but I saw her face was quickly becoming an interesting shade of scarlet.

"If Dexter idolized Trey, why would he kill him?" asked Victoria Vance, a thirty-seven-year-old romance author and my best friend.

"I'm not saying he killed Trey, but keep in mind Dexter was in his final year of undergraduate work at Boston College at the time Trey died. The guy's really smart. I bet by the time he was twenty-two he must have realized his own worth and grown out of his need to idolize an athletic bully. Again, I only spoke to each of the people on my list for a brief time to get a general background, but it seems to me that by the time that party rolled around, Dexter should have been well past the point of being happy being someone's lapdog."

"So you think he could have drugged Trey to get back at him for the way he treated him in high school?" Victoria asked.

"I'm not ready to say that, but Dexter would have had a legitimate complaint, and he's one of the few people on the list who could have had the knowledge to put together the drug cocktail the police believe ended up killing Trey."

Everyone paused to let that sink in. While it was true you could get almost any information on the Web these days, it sounded like the drugs that killed Trey were pretty specific. I wondered if anyone else on the list had a background in chemistry or medicine, so I asked the question.

"Actually, yes. There's another person on the list with the expertise to concoct such a drug cocktail. Her name is Quinn Jenkins, but let me circle back around to her. First, I want to mention Coach Cranston."

"The baseball coach over at the high school?" Jack asked.

"Yes. Coach Cranston has been the coach for a number of years and was Trey's coach when he was in high school," Alex said.

"Trey was a star. Cranston must have loved him."

Alex nodded to Jack. "He did then. In fact, he put in a lot of extra time helping Trey hone his skills. He even managed to get him recognition from other coaches he knew in other parts of the country. The problem was, Trey more or less promised Coach Cranston that if he helped him get a college scholarship, he would take Cranston with him when he went pro. He promised to make him his agent. But when the time came to look for an adviser, he decided he needed someone flashier, someone with more experience. It was while he was home on spring break that he told Cranston he'd decided to go a different way."

"I bet he was angry," Clara Kline, a sixty-two-year-old self-proclaimed psychic and the writer of fantasy and paranormal mysteries, commented.

"From what I've heard, he was. Very angry. He'd stayed in contact with Trey all through his college career, treated him like a son, and discussed their plans for the future on many occasions. Trey's announcement that he was going with someone he'd just met seemed to come from out of left field. I understand Coach Cranston was not only angry but hurt as well."

"Have you considered a scenario where they *all* conspired to drug him?" I asked as the grudges against Trey piled up fast.

"Hang on; I haven't even gotten to the best suspects yet."

"Okay, spill," Brit encouraged. "Who do you think had the strongest reason to kill Trey Alderman?"

"Two other baseball players come to mind. Both were at the party, both played in the charity game during which Trey died, and both improved in ranking with Trey's death. Jett Strong attended Florida State University and was nationally ranked number two behind Trey. The rivalry between Jett and Trey was fierce, and each felt they deserved the title of MVP. During their four years of college, the two traded the number one spot a few times, but as of the day Trey died, it looked like he was going to edge out his rival and come out on top."

"And did Jett finish number one once Trey was out of the picture?" I asked.

"He did."

I jotted down a few notes. "You said there were two rivals?"

"Parker Wilson was the other one. He attended the University of South Carolina with Trey and was his teammate. He was a very good player in his own right, but he couldn't quite compete with Trey, who always stole the spotlight. Many people felt if Parker had been on a different team he would have been a star, but as Trey's teammate, he never got the attention he deserved."

"I bet that sucked," Brit said.

"I'm sure it did," Alex agreed.

"Why didn't Parker just transfer to another school?" I asked.

"It isn't that easy to transfer once you're committed to a sports program, plus he was attending the university on a scholarship," Alex explained.

"Now, what about this Quinn you were going to circle back to?" Brit asked.

Alex shuffled through his notes. "Quinn Jenkins also attended the University of South Carolina and was Parker's girlfriend. An assertive woman majoring in microbiology who felt Parker was getting a raw deal, she wasn't afraid to let anyone who would listen know about it. There are people I've interviewed who felt Quinn was exactly the kind of person to remove obstacles in her way, no matter what it took. For the rest of the season following Trey's death, Parker became the star of the team and was drafted by the New York Yankees. I understand he's building a pretty spectacular career with Quinn at his side."

I completed my notes, then took a step back from the whiteboard. We really had a daunting task ahead of us.

"Do you have a plan?" George asked.

"I know you're all busy with your own lives and careers, so I thought maybe you could tackle the suspects who live on the island, while I go after the ones who live out of state. Parker and Quinn live in New York, which is where I plan to start."

"And Jett?" I asked. "Was he drafted?"

"Yes; to the Florida Marlins. The season is over, so I'm not sure whether he'll be in Florida, but I'll track him down."

"And Rena?" I asked.

"She moved to New York to pursue her modeling career. I'll catch her at the same time I visit Parker and Quinn. I'm planning to leave for New York tomorrow. I'd love to get the interviews and other research wrapped up before Thanksgiving if possible."

"Okay; I'm game to jump right in," I said to the group.

"Me too," Jack seconded.

"I'll consult my cards," Clara promised. "I think this is going to be a juicy one. I can already sense lies and deceit. If I had to guess, the true motive behind Trey's death is still buried deep beneath the surface of the cruelty and betrayal he left behind. Agatha," Clara said, referring to her cat, "thinks there may be another player not yet identified."

"Please have Agatha let us know as soon as she figures out who we're missing," Alex said gently.

"Oh, I will, dear. This is quite a task you're taking on and we're happy to help. Aren't we, Agatha?"

"Meow," answered the cat, sitting primly in Clara's lap.

"And I'll dig in with my research," George promised. "I have several ideas already."

"I'll build a social media map," Brit offered. "I've found them to come in handy."

"I don't know how I can help, but I'm in as well," Victoria offered.

"Great," I said after everyone had chimed in. I looked at Blackbeard, my very opinionated and very intuitive parrot, who seemed to be able to communicate his thoughts and feelings. "How about it, big guy? You up for another mystery?"

Blackbeard didn't respond, which was uncharacteristic of him.

I turned back to the others, "I guess he doesn't have anything to say. Can everyone meet back here on Monday evening? That will give us time to do some digging around."

Everyone agreed Monday would be fine. Jack was going to make some calls the next day, and then he and I would get started with interviews on Friday. Hopefully, once we began speaking to people a pattern would emerge.

"Before everyone goes, I wanted to give you an update on the cabin situation," I said. "The inspector is coming tomorrow and I expect we'll receive the permits for the second three cabins." I looked directly at Victoria. "I know you plan to move into the largest of the three, but that still leaves two cabins I need to find tenants for." I turned toward Clara. "Are you sure you'd prefer to stay in the main house?"

"Yes, dear. Agatha and I are quite happy in our room on the second floor."

"Okay, then, I'll look for tenants for the other two cabins. I have a woman coming by tomorrow for an interview. Her name is Harper Carrington and she's a true crime writer. I'm not certain she's interested in a long-term rental; so far, she's expressed interest in leasing a cabin for a few months while she does research in this area. I feel as if we're a family, so I wanted to be sure no one has had any negative experiences with her. I understand she can be assertive."

"Never heard of her," Brit said.

"I've never met her but I've read her work," George offered. "She seems to be committed to telling the victim's story in much the way we do here. I found her research and conclusions to be thorough and well thought out. I have a feeling she'll fit in just fine."

I looked around at the others. "Anyone else have an opinion?"

No one spoke up, so I decided to go ahead with the interview to get a firsthand impression.

"Okay, then; I guess that's all I have." I glanced at Victoria. "You should be able to begin moving in tomorrow afternoon."

"Great. Who want to help me move my stuff over?"

Everyone except Alex, who would be gone by then, agreed to help. Shortly after the group began to break up. I walked Jack to the door, then came back in to clean up.

"So what do you think?" Alex asked as I put away the dry erase markers I'd been using for the whiteboard.

"I think the mystery is intriguing and I believe the others are hooked as well, but I do need to ask why you decided to write this specific book. You usually write science fiction. A biography seems out of your wheelhouse."

Alex shrugged. "I'm not really sure what prompted me to write this book. I'm interested in sports, and Trey's story was one that caught national attention at the time of his death. The whole thing seemed odd to me, so I did some digging and realized

I wanted to follow the clues wherever they might lead."

"Well, I'm glad you brought the mystery to the group. I've found working as a team to be quite satisfying."

"I'm glad you're in. I'm going to head out early in the morning, so I guess I'll see you on Sunday, or Monday afternoon at the latest."

"Call me in a day or two to touch base."

"I will. I'm hoping we'll have the suspect list narrowed down a bit by this time next week."

I hoped Alex was right, though I'd found that when it came to researching cold cases, things were never as simple as they might initially seem.

Once everyone had gone off to their own cabin or room, I wrapped myself in a heavy sweater and headed out onto the deck. It was a clear night and the stars shone brightly in the dark sky. I sat down on one of the patio chairs and closed my eyes. I loved listening to the sound of the waves rolling onto the shore. I felt the tension melt from my body as the gentle rhythm eased the stress created by a phone call from my mother earlier in the day. I'd hoped she would agree to come to the island for Thanksgiving. She had yet to see my new home or meet my new friends. I also really wanted her to meet Garrett, the half brother with whom I shared a father, even though I knew it was going to be a sensitive subject to address.

Of course, even though Mom admitted she wasn't busy over Thanksgiving, she made it clear she was much *too* busy to come to my little island. She invited me to fly out to join her in Los Angeles, but spending Thanksgiving with her Hollywood crowd sounded like the worst idea I'd heard in quite some time. There was no doubt about it; I'd just need to have my own dinner. Not that I had a clue where to start in preparing such a meal. Gertie Newsome, owner of Gertie's on the Wharf, had attended my Halloween dinner party; maybe she'd agree not only to spend Thanksgiving at the Turtle Cove Writers' Retreat but help with the planning and cooking as well.

"Beautiful night," I heard George say.

I opened my eyes. "It is. Are you out for a walk?"

"A short one. Walking helps to clear my mind so I can settle in without a million thoughts running through my head, disturbing my sleep. Mind if I sit with you for a minute?"

"Not at all. I'd welcome the company."

George sat down next to me. He took the old pipe he often smoked out of his pocket and held it up in question. I nodded, so he lit it and took a few puffs of the sweet-smelling tobacco. I wasn't a fan of cigarette or even cigar smoke, but I found the smoke from a pipe brought back fond memories of my grandfather.

George and I sat in silence for a few minutes before he spoke. "I was down at the museum today, talking to Meg about the history of the island for the historical novel I'm writing."

He paused, and it seemed to me his thought was incomplete. "How did that go?" I asked.

"Good. Meg is a very bright woman. She had a lot of very useful information and she seemed very enthusiastic about sharing her love of the island. She really is quite remarkable."

"She is," I agreed.

"I was wondering if you knew much about her personal life."

I turned and looked directly at George. “Her personal life?”

“Marital status. That sort of thing.”

I smiled. It looked as if George might have a crush on the turtle rescue lady. “I know she’s currently single and that she has a daughter who lives out of state, so I imagine she must have been married at some point, although it’s possible to have a child without a husband. She’s lived on the island for a long time; I’ve had conversations with her in which she’s shared memories of events that occurred here decades ago. I also know she’s kind and intelligent and really cares about the island, the people who live here, and the turtles she protects.”

“So you’re certain she isn’t currently involved in a romantic relationship?”

I placed my hand on George’s arm. “No, I’m not certain. The subject’s never come up between us, but based on what I’ve observed, I’d say she’s very much single. If you want to know for certain, why don’t you ask her?”

It was odd to see George, who was always so confident and levelheaded stuttering around like a schoolboy.

“I’ve had a good life though I’ve never married and really haven’t dated all that much. The pursuit of knowledge has always been my mistress, so asking out a woman I’ve only recently gotten to know feels awkward. Maybe I should just spend more time at the museum. Get to know her better.”

“That’s probably a good idea. I’m thinking of having a big Thanksgiving dinner here at the resort. I haven’t asked everyone yet, but I am fairly certain everyone plans to be around. Why don’t you invite her? I don't know whether she already has plans, but if she doesn't, it'll give you the opportunity to get that first date out of the way while surrounded by people who know and love you."

George furrowed his brow. I could see he needed to give the idea some thought. "It would be a nice thing to invite her to have Thanksgiving with all of us if she doesn't have plans. I've spent a good number of holidays alone, and I can say from experience that being by yourself while others are with family and friends is a lonely proposition."

"I agree. Meg knows everyone at the retreat to a certain degree and I'm sure she would be happy to have a place to go if she isn't already busy."

"Okay." I could see George had made up his mind. "I'll ask her tomorrow."

"Great. I'm going to invite all the writers here, along with Jack and Gertie, who I'm hoping will help with the cooking. Oh, and Deputy Savage, although he has family on the island, so he may be busy."

George chuckled. "Oh, I don't know about that. Judging by the way he and Victoria eye each other when they think no one is looking, I'd say there's a good chance he'll come if she'll be here."

George had a point. Deputy Rick Savage and Victoria had been tiptoeing around each other ever since she'd been back from Los Angeles, and I suspected it was only a matter of time before the cat-and-mouse dance they'd been engaged in turned into another sort of dance entirely.

Books by Kathi Daley

Come for the murder, stay for the romance.

Zoe Donovan Cozy Mystery:

Halloween Hijinks
The Trouble With Turkeys
Christmas Crazy
Cupid's Curse
Big Bunny Bump-off
Beach Blanket Barbie
Maui Madness
Derby Divas
Haunted Hamlet
Turkeys, Tuxes, and Tabbies
Christmas Cozy
Alaskan Alliance
Matrimony Meltdown
Soul Surrender
Heavenly Honeymoon
Hopscotch Homicide
Ghostly Graveyard
Santa Sleuth
Shamrock Shenanigans
Kitten Kaboodle
Costume Catastrophe
Candy Cane Caper
Holiday Hangover
Easter Escapade
Camp Carter
Trick or Treason – *September 2017*
Reindeer Roundup – *December 2017*

Zimmerman Academy The New Normal
Ashton Falls Cozy Cookbook

Tj Jensen Paradise Lake Mysteries by Henery Press

Pumpkins in Paradise
Snowmen in Paradise
Bikinis in Paradise
Christmas in Paradise
Puppies in Paradise
Halloween in Paradise
Treasure in Paradise
Fireworks in Paradise – *October 2017*

Whales and Tails Cozy Mystery:

Romeow and Juliet
The Mad Catter
Grimm's Furry Tail
Much Ado About Felines
Legend of Tabby Hollow
Cat of Christmas Past
A Tale of Two Tabbies
The Great Catsby
Count Catula
The Cat of Christmas Present
A Winter's Tail
The Taming of the Tabby
Frankencat – *August 2017*
The Cat of Christmas Future – *November 2017*

Seacliff High Mystery:

The Secret
The Curse
The Relic
The Conspiracy
The Grudge
The Shadow
The Haunting – *September 2017*

Sand and Sea Hawaiian Mystery:

Murder at Dolphin Bay
Murder at Sunrise Beach
Murder at the Witching Hour
Murder at Christmas
Murder at Turtle Cove
Murder at Water's Edge
Murder at Midnight – *October 2017*

Writers' Retreat Southern Seashore Mystery:

First Case
Second Look
Third Strike
Fourth Victim – *October 2017*

Rescue Alaska Paranormal Mystery

Finding Justice – *November 2017*

Road to Christmas Romance:

Road to Christmas Past

USA Today bestselling author, Kathi Daley, lives in beautiful Lake Tahoe with her husband Ken. When she isn't writing, she likes spend time hiking the miles of desolate trails surrounding her home. She has authored more than seventy five books in eight series including: Zoe Donovan Cozy Mysteries, Whales and Tails Island Mysteries, Sand and Sea Hawaiian Mysteries, Tj Jensen Paradise Lake Series, Writer's Retreat Southern Seashore Mysteries, Rescue Alaska Paranormal Mysteries, and Seacliff High Teen Mysteries. Find out more about her books at **www.kathidaley.com**

Giveaway:

I do a giveaway for books, swag, and gift cards every week in my newsletter, *The Daley Weekly* **http://eepurl.com/NRPDf**

Other links to check out:

Kathi Daley Blog – publishes each Friday
http://kathidaleyblog.com

Webpage – **www.kathidaley.com**

Facebook at Kathi Daley Books –
www.facebook.com/kathidaleybooks

Kathi Daley Teen – **www.facebook.com/kathidaleyteen**

Kathi Daley Books Group Page –
https://www.facebook.com/groups/569578823146850/

E-mail – **kathidaley@kathidaley.com**

Goodreads –
https://www.goodreads.com/author/show/7278377.Kathi_Daley

Twitter at Kathi Daley@kathidaley –
https://twitter.com/kathidaley

Amazon Author Page –
https://www.amazon.com/author/kathidaley

BookBub – **https://www.bookbub.com/authors/kathi-daley**

Pinterest – **http://www.pinterest.com/kathidaley/**

CPSIA information can be obtained
at www.ICGtesting.com
Printed in the USA
LVHW04s1248120618
580436LV00029B/394/P